Deranged

BWWM Dark Bully Romance

The Crispin & Amina Series
Book 4

Jamila Jasper

Edited by
Rosie M

Content Notice

The content in this story may be disturbing to some readers. Sensitive readers beware, this is a dark BWWM bully romance novel with themes readers may find troubling and frank discussions about race that may disturb some readers.

Violence, strong language, potentially offensive content, sexual violence and death are all mentioned explicitly in this story.

This is a hot, slow-burn interracial romance story in an interconnected series.

Dive into my most popular serial, completely updated for readers who enjoy and prefer completed full-length novels.

**This book was previously published as a Kindle Vella story and will
now be updated completely and published as an eBook. The story line,
characters and structure will be updated and edited for the eBook
format.**

**Please read this warning before purchasing this book or going any
further.**

❀ Created with Vellum

Deranged

Dark BWWM Billionaire Bully Romance

Book #4

The Crispin & Amina Series

Description

"This was a deal breaker. Killing and stabbing women was a deal breaker. That was normal..."

Amina finds her boyfriend in a compromising position.

His love for her reaches an extreme when he yields to his sociopathic tendencies.

Given Amina's past, she runs for the hills.

Crispin, the billionaire heir who pledged to love her forever, won't let her disappear so easily.

As Amina's trust unravels and Crispin's obsession reaches new heights, their love story only becomes more deranged...

This is Book #4 in a series of dark interracial enemies to lovers bully romance books. If you enjoy spicy romance

books that contain potentially triggering and offensive content with page-turning plots and addictive kindle-burning smuttiness, you will fall in love with this series.

This is a series of interconnected books about Crispin & Amina. I suggest beginning from Book #1.

Chapter One

Do you remember where you left us? I hope you do because Crispin and I were entangled in something big. Something I hope you wouldn't forget.

I was at a party with my boyfriend – the devastatingly handsome boarding college football star and billionaire heir Crispin Barclay – when he disappeared.

I desperately searched everywhere for him until I wandered outside, and heard a woman's loud scream.

I FOUND CRISPIN, my boyfriend, holding my worst enemy half-naked, captive, and tied to a tree...

CRISPIN HAD her tied against a tree — tightly. I knew that man could tie a knot and he'd tied several around Ella Novak's body. She was half undressed. He'd clearly cut off some of her clothing and hit her. *Hard*. Ella was pale, so even in the darkness, I could make out the bruised parts of her flesh.

Despite Ella's screaming, Crispin was quiet and scarily calm. He was too fixated on her to notice me approaching or watching. He flipped the knife I'd given him for Christmas between his fingers and as he stared at Ella. She screamed again and he slowly ran his index finger lightly along the sharp edge of the blade as he watched her.

He was so focused on whatever he planned that he didn't hear me stomping my way down the moor. As I ran closer to them, I saw the hateful expression on his face. *He's going to kill her.* Panic surged through me as I raced closer. By then, he should have been able to hear me approaching, but he was so damn obsessed with his task that he didn't break eye contact with Ella.

"Crispin! What are you doing?" I yelled.

I could tell he was surprised by my arrival down the rolling green hill because he bristled. But he made it a point not to turn around. I couldn't bear to look at Ella.

"Go away, Amina. I'm *communicating* with Ella."

"He cut me!" She screamed.

I reluctantly looked at her closely for the first time since running down the hill. She couldn't move any of her limbs the way Crispin had her tied up. He cut her jeans open with his knife and then made a small two inch long cut on her leg. He'd cut her shirt in several places and there was blood soaking through and a dark bruise on her shoulder. Blood dribbled down her thigh and coated the blade of Crispin's new knife. My throat tightened.

Terror. I'd never felt terror when encountering Crispin's dark side but this was worse than I'd ever seen him. Far worse. He didn't even look at me or seem to notice me. There was a frenetic bloodlust in his eye that rendered me invisible. *Don't worry, white boy. If you won't look at me, I can yell.*

"Crispin... seriously. What the hell are you doing?"

"I am ensuring your safety."

"You're a monster!" Ella yelled.

Crispin rolled his eyes.

"Don't be melodramatic, Ella. I gave you a choice. Drop out of Rapetti Academy or suffer. You dumped John. Splendid. But that's not enough."

I grabbed onto Crispin's forearm, pleading with him not to do this. Don't hurt her. Don't *kill her.* Bile rose in my throat, but I couldn't make myself do anything other than tug on his arm. He didn't push me off, but he didn't turn to look at me either. He said in a deep, terrifying voice again, "Go away, Amina."

"She's not worth this. She's not worth getting in trouble."

"Believe me, I won't get in trouble."

"He's going to rape me!" Ella sobbed.

"Don't flatter yourself," Crispin snarled at her.

I hit him. *Hard.*

"Crispin! Stop it! I want to go inside. You're freaking me out. I get it, you want revenge but it's not like you're going to kill her."

He pulled away from me and then met my eyes. I finally saw it. He *was* going to kill her. That was exactly what he'd planned. He couldn't just get it done with... he *needed more.*

He was torturing her too. Crispin seriously wanted to kill Ella Novak for me. I wanted to feel loathing and disgust for him, but I couldn't condemn him completely. His heart was in the right place. I appreciated how much he wanted to do

3

for me but how that ended up with murder in Crispin's twisted mind scared the crap out of me. *Why do I like it, though? Why do I love everything he does even when it scares me?*

"You gave me the knife," he said. "I understand what you want from me."

"You think I want you to murder my friend?"

"I'm not your friend, you lying slut!" Ella yelled, with little sense for self-preservation. Luckily, unlike my boyfriend, I wasn't a sociopath.

"Shut the fuck up, Ella. Seriously, just because I don't want him to stab you, doesn't mean you're not dumb as fuck."

Ella sniffled and then sobbed.

"They're going to kill me and rape me…" she whimpered, to no one in particular, as if she was conducting a True Crime narration of her own life.

Crispin's eyes were still fixed on me.

"Let me do what I must," he said, seriously. "I need this… I need to do this for you."

His excitement made me wonder if he was doing this for me or for his own dark needs. I knew Crispin had dark needs. I just didn't know how far he would go to express those needs. My palms were slick as I tried to come up with convincing arguments that could pierce through Crispin's emotional reasoning and untamed bloodlust.

"You can't kill her. You *seriously* can't."

"Why not?" he said. "Everyone already thinks I'm a killer. I can handle it."

No. I didn't want him to become that person. Ella might have been a terrible person, but I didn't need her to die.

"Because it's wrong," I pleaded with Crispin.

4

He shrugged. "Hurting you is wrong."

"It's not the same!"

"I don't want to argue with you. I planned this out. I'll handle this, get cleaned up and then... I present you a symbol of my love and we have sex all night."

"We're a few seconds away from midnight and you're going to make me miss it because you're knifing Ella Novak!"

He seemed genuinely confused at how upset I was. We could hear people counting down to midnight and the party's energy changing back at the house.

"This is more important than a kiss. I kiss you plenty."

Ella whimpered loudly again and then made a gagging noise in her throat which she thought was far more subtle than it really was.

I grabbed his forearm and pleaded with him, "You can't kill her."

"What do you want me to do then?"

"Let her go. And warn her that if she fucks with me again, I won't stop you."

I didn't know if I meant it or if I just wanted him to stop. I tried to sound genuine so he wouldn't call my bluff. The pause was painful. But then Crispin dropped the knife and sighed with relief.

"If you'd just go away, you wouldn't have anything to worry about."

"Except guilt and remorse."

His jaw shifted forward and then back again. Frustration. *Fine, be frustrated.* I didn't care what he did or felt as long as he didn't kill her. I didn't want him to become everyone's worst fears. I didn't want him to be... *evil.*

5

"I'd do anything you commanded. I don't know why you won't let me do this."

He glanced over at her and stuck a cigarette between his lips before slowly cutting her free with a serrated knife. Ella was shaking and far too wobbly to run away. Crispin didn't care. He pushed her and she fell over.

"Novak," he snarled as she hit the ground with a thud and a loud yelp. "One day my girlfriend won't be here to stop me. And then I swear, I'll do what I planned."

"You're a freak! You're both fucking freaks!"

Crispin shrugged.

"Maybe. But at least I'm not desperate. Think of who you fear more, Novak. Me or John Hewett. I bet I'm less of a fucking pussy. Choose wisely."

Crispin was definitely taking it too far. I shot Ella an apologetic look. She sneered at me, and then her legs and senses seemed to kick in and she scrambled up to her feet and ran. Crispin turned back towards his knife, unconcerned. I was still angry with him. Furious. My body trembled as I realized that it wasn't just that he scared me. This was a deal-breaker. Killing and stabbing women was a dealbreaker. I think that's normal.

"Hurry. We need to talk about this."

"I need my knife."

A surge of rage flooded me. All he cared about was blood, his knife and his stupid trophies. He didn't even notice how freaked out I was.

He picked the knife up and wiped the blood off with a handkerchief. I wrinkled my nose in disgust as he stuck it back in his pocket.

"This is way too far Crispin."

"Is it?"

He lit the cigarette as he walked slowly toward the house.

"Yes! I mean... do you even care about the fact that it's New Year?"

"No. I don't."

"But you care about stabbing Ella Novak and God knows what else. Were you going to rape her?"

He stopped suddenly and raised an eyebrow, puffing annoyingly on his cigarette.

"Do you worry that I desire her?"

"No! That's not what I asked..." I said. I wanted to push him. I wanted to tell him about Frances calling me but I also wanted to punch him in the face. It was complicated.

"I wouldn't rape her or anyone. And I don't want *her*. I want you."

He couldn't see how this would scare me. How I wouldn't see it as a pure expression of his love. Crispin's eyes were fiery with defiance and I wanted to go crazy and slap the hell out of his perfect face. His jawline was so chiseled I could cut my hand on it, but I wanted to risk it all and hit him.

"Funny way you have of showing that you want me," I snapped at him. His face fell. I hated his disappointment. I was the one who found him with a girl tied to a tree. I was the one who spent half the night looking for him.

All I wanted was for tonight to be special. To mean something to us. Crispin shrugged and my hopes for the night spiraled into a meaningless heap in front of me that Crispin appeared unaware of entirely.

"We're going to miss the countdown," Crispin said. "We might as well give up and quit fussing over it."

"Are you kidding me?" I said, annoyed by myself for

sounding so American and also like I was nagging him. When did our perfect love story turn into this? *Maybe it was never so perfect?*

He stopped suddenly, his body tensing with anger. I flinched instinctively, even if I knew Crispin would never hurt me. But he just snapped at me so coldly that I couldn't help but feel a sharp stabbing sensation twisting my insides up.

"Damn it, Amina. Maybe I don't care about this countdown, New Year, or bloody anything at all."

Then I got angry. Really angry. I hated his apathy and his violence. I hated how he disappointed me when all I wanted was to spend New Year's Eve with him. *And kiss him.* I hated how he could be so goddamn stubborn and unpredictable. I wanted him to feel what I felt.

"You know what, Crispin? I'm so done."

"Done with what?"

"You aren't even listening to me tonight. All I want is a normal night with my boyfriend and you're off avenging me like a terrifying... like a *murderer*."

"Don't you already know that I'm a killer?" he said softly. "Doesn't a part of you believe it?"

I stopped and folded my arms. I didn't want to get close to him. Not now. I didn't know if I'd ever want to get close to him again. It was dark and eerily quiet aside from the distant party. I never feared being alone with Crispin but I couldn't help the instinctive knot forming in my gut or the way the hairs on the back of my neck stood up.

"What are you saying? Is this a confession?"

He looked terribly sad for a moment and my stomach lurched. It was so goddamn cold and creepy out here. I wrapped my arms around myself as I stared at him, hoping to find answers on his face. All I could see was what little light there was reflecting off his eyes, making them look translucent.

"Crispin Barclay. Have you lied to me about anything?"

He answered me quickly. Too quickly.

"Yes," he said. "But it's not about what you think."

I made a loud anguished sound that sounded inhuman and didn't feel like it came from inside me. He didn't feel like the Crispin I loved anymore after what I'd nearly seen him do. I could handle when he told people off, but the way he seemed to delight in violence terrified me. What if one day he turned that dark side toward me and I'd become the girl, tied to a tree and bleeding from her thigh. Crispin wanted to lunge at me. I sensed it. But I also sensed he knew I would run.

He waited for me to speak.

"You're scaring me," I whispered, hating how pathetic I sounded after my frustrated howling-grunt noise. I just wanted to hit him and that frustration was all I could do to stop myself from doing something stupid.

"Haven't I always scared you?" he whispered. His voice sounded low and dangerous. My heart raced faster. I feared his lies more than his violence. How could he hold back from me when I couldn't hold anything back from him? It just wasn't fair.

"That's not an excuse," I replied weakly.

"*Sweetheart...*"

"Don't call me that," I snapped. "Don't call me anything. I can hear them counting down inside..."

We were quiet for a moment. I was utterly torn.

"I'll kiss you out here," he said. "Please."

"No," I said. "I don't want you to kiss me. I don't want to be in this relationship."

"What?" He said, trying to hide how hurt he was. I hated myself for having to hurt him like this. For having to end things with him.

I lowered my gaze and said, "I don't want to hurt you."

"Hurt me? You're bloody serious?"

Now he sounded... *anguished.*

I continued babbling, my mouth getting ahead of me, "I don't want you to hurt people for me. I don't... I can't bear thinking that you're a monster. I can't. I love you too much. But when I see you acting like that it reminds me— ."

"Don't say it," he murmured, "Don't."

"It reminds me of *him.*"

Crispin froze for a moment. Then he pushed hair out of his face and he was calm, but not remorseful.

"Not all killers are monsters," he said. "Some people kill out of loyalty. Or for justice."

"It's not up to us to determine what that is," I said. "It's not up to you."

"But sometimes it is, Amina."

I snapped, "What are you trying to tell me?'

4...

3...

2...

1...

Crispin didn't approach me.

"I'll go to Jack and Vi's tonight to give you time to think. Have fun with your friends. I'm not going to let you break up with me out here. We'll talk."

"Okay fine," I said, ignoring the bigger pit in my stomach. Crispin was a monster. What I'd seen him doing to Ella was scary. The fact that he couldn't tell why it was wrong was scarier. And then the lies. What else was he lying about...

Fireworks. Well, fireworks outside. Our relationship was totally dead. At least that's what it felt like. I was scared and hollow and I felt this nagging feeling that Crispin had been trying to admit something important to me. He'd lied about something and judging by what I'd seen tonight, it was probably about one of the several murders associated with him.

"If you want me to come back before we head to Rapetti, text me. If not, I'll give you space. I'm sorry if I've fucked things up. And... I'm sorry that I still have secrets. I just want you to know that if I have secrets from you, it's because I want to protect you."

"That's not a good enough reason."

His face softened.

"I would do anything to protect you, Twiggy. I would do so many fucked up things to keep you safe."

I wanted to run to him, but my instincts were telling me Crispin was dangerous.

"I'll make sure you get to Glottenham safe," he whispered, "And then I'll leave. I don't want to spoil your night. And if any other guy in our year touches you, I'll castrate him. I don't share. And I'll never share you."

A chill ran down my spine. After what I'd seen tonight, I finally believed in Crispin's darkness. He didn't even seem to care about how badly he'd scared me this time and how it was different from everything else. I wanted his love and protection, but I didn't want it to feel like the familiar terrifying control I'd felt growing up in the governor's mansion.

11

He walked me to the door of Glottenham. In the outdoor lights, I saw his cheeks red from the cold and his eyes red and slightly wet. The noise from the party grew louder as we grew closer. I could feel myself leaving the little world we'd built together that was just the two of us.

The numbness that always took hold in my chest and in the base of my stomach when I felt strong emotions returned. It was the worst type of pain to want to turn to the person who hurt you for comfort from the same hurt.

"I don't feel sorry for hurting her," he said, "But I feel sorry for hurting you."

"Crispin..."

This time, he lunged for me, grabbing my hips and then pressing me against the door. He was enormous and firm and he wanted me. Against my better judgment, I let him kiss me and we might not have kissed right at midnight, but we kissed *a lot*. The painful goodbye kisses made me want to cry, but I knew that I couldn't. I just had to enjoy Crispin's lips and his firm, enormous body.

He pulled away from me and with an anguished look on his face he muttered, "I'd better go."

Crispin disappeared into the night. My stomach tightened nervously. Had I made a huge mistake?

Chapter Two

I never called Crispin or texted him to come back to Glottenham. I'd been serious about needing to think and I'd been serious about how badly he'd scared me. I didn't have a clue what happened to Ella after the attack. Crispin wasn't in prison as far as I knew, so she hadn't told anyone. I didn't like comparing him to John Hewett.

I knew that probably hurt him. *Sigh*.

I was just... scared. Traumatized, maybe? The terror of what I'd seen in him and then his half-confession worried me. Ben and Libby were curious about what was wrong and they didn't make me feel unwelcome at all. But I still worried that I had blown everything out of proportion. It was just my gut twisted in knots every time I thought of the look in Crispin's eye. He was seriously going to kill her. I knew he wanted to.

Ben asked me if I needed him to talk some sense into Crispin... with a cricket bat and Theo offered to mediate with a "peace pipe". Libby tried to tell them that we needed to sort this out on our own. But she was a good friend too.

When I woke up one morning crying because I missed him after only a few days, she sat with me and listened to me for a while. She never told me what to do, she just listened. She *cared*.

"It's hard to love someone with that darkness in them," she whispered, touching my back gently like the big sister I never had.

"It worked out for you," I whispered. "Didn't it?"

From what I'd heard about Ben and Libby so far, they had their fair share of ups and downs. Libby smiled meekly, but only offered encouraging words, not details. I guess we weren't like Ben and Libby. We weren't meant to be.

I nearly called Crispin that day but then... *I couldn't.*

ELLA HAD LEFT the party on the night of the incident and she hadn't told anyone what happened according to my sources, but that didn't change the look I'd seen in Crispin's eyes. The look that told me he'd *killed before*. And then he'd practically confessed. The worst part about us being "secret friends" before getting together was that I knew him too well. I knew when he was lying to me now and the fact that he still was hurt like hell.

My time in Ben and Libby's mansion went by slowly. Ben and Libby tried to entertain me and they brought Theo in when they were too busy to spend time with me. The last person I needed to babysit me was Crispin's cousin, who I suspected was spying on me.

Theo was a good sport about it. He brought me weed whenever I wanted, had good tastes in music and he never made a move on me. I enjoyed hanging out with him.

. . .

WHEN IT WAS time for me to go back to campus, I seriously had no clue how I would get there. Libby organized everything for me in advance before I even had to ask about it.

Theo drove me to Rapetti. He tried to convince me to talk to Crispin but I didn't want to speak to Crispin anymore.

"He's a lover, you know?" Theo kept repeating, like that justified Crispin tying a girl up and threatening her life. He kept defending Crispin after he heard what happened. I would have preferred if Theo didn't find out, but we smoked a little too much weed one night and I found my secrets just spilling out during our heart to heart.

When I insisted I wouldn't take Crispin back under any circumstances, red-faced Theo tried to politely change the subject to Libby and Ben's upcoming baby. He wanted to work out if Ben would name the baby after him but he didn't want Ben to worry that he'd fathered the child. Theo was sweet but... I didn't think Ben Fox would be threatened by him. No way. Libby was clearly crazy about Ben.

Vi promised she'd meet me after I moved in. There were only a few girls switching rooms at the change of the semester, and being back at Rapetti again felt... *strange*. I hadn't messaged Crispin back in days.

CRISPIN: I miss you, Twiggy
   Crispin: I love you.

. . .

15

I THINK that was pretty much it. We were finished. I was single again and ready to mingle. Ugh... Who was I kidding. I didn't want to mingle with anyone. I couldn't. I'd broken up with Crispin but... I still loved him.

Why couldn't I just go back to him? It was a New Year, and I wanted to be more grown up. To not just follow my instincts if they were going to lead me into more danger. I didn't want to end up like Frances. Hell, I didn't want to end up living with the fear I'd grown up with.

I just needed to trust him again before I could go back to him. For the first time ever, love wasn't enough between us.

Loving him made me feel so damn stupid sometimes. Because I still wanted us to be fixed. He made me feel too trusting. *Fairy girl.* Maybe boys think fairies are weak. Maybe that's what he thought about me.

I slowly unpacked my suitcases, folding my underwear one at a time without hitting up any of the heavier boxes with my decorations or big black sweaters.

I dreaded plenty of people more than I dreaded seeing Crispin or even Ella Novak. I didn't want to see Katrina again. Vi and I had sworn not to admit that we knew about her pregnancy. We wanted to find out if she'd changed at all... if she'd finally get honest with us.

Mandeep's side of the room was already unpacked. She had a poster of Freddie Mercury framed over her desk and boxes of incense. I tried to look around her room and figure out what sort of girl she was. I didn't even care that she'd offered to give Crispin a blowjob. Whatever, my man had a nice dick. Well, I guess he wasn't *my* man anymore. But his dick was still nice.

I'd heard mixed comments about Mandeep. Her room

seemed normal and girly, and the heavy woody scent of her expensive perfume filled the air, even if she'd clearly been gone for hours. She'd made her bed, which probably meant she was neat. All her clothes smelled like expensive perfume that wafted off of them whenever she moved and she had a little bottle of vodka sitting on the desk.

Mandeep was terrifying, according to Vi Bainbridge. Vi told me everything on the phone our last night before coming back to school when I couldn't sleep because I missed Crispin. It was painful. I could hear him playing beer pong with Jack in the background and I missed him. I missed his crazy ass so much. But I had to protect myself from Crispin.

I didn't want him hurting people and I didn't want him hurting women... even women like Ella Novak. I hated her and I thought she was *terrible*, but that didn't mean she deserved Crispin looming over her making her *think* he might rape or kill her.

That was pure evil. I hated thinking that Crispin was pure evil. Vi's gossip turned in my head as I stared at Mandeep's family picture framed on her desk.

Mandeep played field hockey and she was one of the fastest girls on the team and the worst at hazing in the locker rooms. Sarah Clifford played field hockey for one week and Mandeep *pinched her nipples so hard that they bled*.

"She's sadistic and she does drugs all the time," Vi admitted.

Where the hell did Vi get all this gossip? Never mind. I knew it was Trevor. The two of them openly reveled in speculation and gossip. Trevor was more prone to outright lying than Violet at least.

"I don't care about that."

17

"She's hardcore. I'd be careful. She'll probably try to get you hooked on coke."

Still, Vi had done enough to scare me. She probably thought she was doing me a favor, preparing me for the move to L.C. When I entered my room, I thought I'd meet Mandeep right away, but I didn't mind the time to do some gentle investigation.

She had a quote written on her mirror. *LOSE FUCKING WEIGHT.*

I grimaced as I looked at it. Wow. Hello, horrible trigger. I dragged my things over to the bed and started unpacking. I put my sheets together and started pulling out clothes. When I opened the closet... *I screamed.*

"What on earth are you doing in here?!" I yelled at him. He was acting like everything between us was just like the old days, but it wasn't. My eyes were bugging out of my head and this time, I didn't know if I could stop myself from smacking the hell out of Crispin.

Crispin stepped out of my closet, rolling his shoulders and shrugging, giving me an impossibly cocky grin like he didn't give a crap about the severity of his crime.

"It's a tight fit."

He yawned and stretched like a giant wildcat and not a bedroom intruder. I folded my arms and gave him my best angry face.

"Um... what are you doing?"

"We haven't spoken in a bloody week. I want to find out how you are. I... I miss you."

"We are broken up," I snapped at him, hitting his shoulders. *Damn.* I didn't know how he became more muscular. I pulled my hand away quickly and tried to stay focused on my outrage. A thick, defined bicep couldn't get in the way of my anger.

"Crispin... you can't break into my room. I haven't even met my roommate yet."

Crispin scowled. "You won't reply to my texts."

"You haven't taken accountability."

"Bloody hell. Where did you learn about that rubbish?"

"It's not rubbish."

He didn't wipe the scowl off his face. His voice just got more stubborn and more annoying. "I'm not letting you dump me like this, Twiggy."

"Why not?" I snapped, popping my hip and letting that white boy know I was ready to fight him for breaking into my room. How did he even find out where I lived and get here first? Vi and Jack weren't getting back to campus until later.

Crispin turned red.

"Because... I love you," he said. His eyes flickered to mine. I could see that he felt sorry for hurting me, but that didn't change anything. Just like his muscles and chiseled jawline didn't change anything.

I loved him too. But that didn't change the darkness Crispin revealed.

"I need time, Crispin," I said. "Please."

"Ben called," Crispin grumbled. "He told me I was an idiot and that I ought to apologize. I agree. I'm an idiot. I took it too far with Ella. I'm not sorry I hurt her... but I'm sorry I hurt you."

Great. Theo must have finally told Ben. I knew he was a chatty patty ass white boy... I folded my arms and tried not to expose my frustration. Or how badly I wanted to take Crispin back and yield to my primal desire for him.

"Okay. Fine. You're sorry. But you need to go before my roommate gets back."

"No."

I stormed over and tried to drag Crispin to the door. He was big. Way too big to let me drag him around like this. He grabbed my shoulders instead and gazed at me.

"I've fucked up. But I didn't come here just to bother you. I have news and I don't have anyone else to tell."

"You can tell me this but you can't tell me your big dark secret..."

"Amina... *please.*"

"Fine. Tell me."

"You were right," he whispered. "John's my family. But... he's not my brother or my half-brother. I think... I think John's my uncle."

"Your grandfather cheated?"

Crispin shrugged.

"I already told you he likes escorts. But John's mum... John's mum had him when she was fifteen."

"Oh," I said... "Ew..."

Crispin licked his lips and shook his head.

"You saw it immediately. Why didn't I?"

"No offense but white people tend to think all black people look the same. You probably didn't notice."

Crispin didn't argue with me, which was a relief. Still, I wasn't sure how I felt about having him back in my room. He turned to me and sighed.

"You still look healthy. I worried about that. Libby muted me in our text message thread because I asked too many questions..."

"I'm fine," I lied. I wasn't. I missed him so much that

having him standing here was making me very confused. His closeness made me want him, no matter how dark he was. I wished I could forget what I'd seen.

"John's my uncle and I don't know what to do about it but... I wanted you to know. Thank you, Lips. You're so... bloody smart."

I wanted to go to him then and wrap my arms around him. But I couldn't bring myself to stop feeling scared of him and what he'd do.

He reached into his pocket and murmured, "I brought you something else."

And because he was Crispin Barclay, naturally, he pulled out a knife. Was this really the best time for him to do this? My heart raced as I gazed at him skeptically. Was he taking me seriously? Or was this about to become another terrifying situation at the hands of a monster...

Chapter Three

He tossed the knife onto my bed. My Christmas present. My heart lurched when I saw it. He noticed the troubled expression on my face and drew closer to me.

"This is your control over me. I won't use it on anyone. Ever. Not unless you command me. I know my dark urges scare you, Lips. But I'll let you control them."

"This doesn't solve things."

His voice was low and gentle. I wanted to allow Crispin's posh English accent to lure me in. "What would?"

"You're not in control, Crispin. If you could do that to Ella, how can I trust you wouldn't hurt me like that?"

"I wouldn't," he said. "I promise. I would only hurt *for* you."

I said what I hadn't been able to say out loud finally and it was hard to admit. Very hard. But Crispin didn't seem to find my concerns terrifying. He moved closer still and I stepped back.

"Did I scare you?" he asked. He was so close to putting

his arm around me. I hated myself for wanting him to wrap me up in a big warm hug again.

I nodded. He bit down on his lower lip so hard that it turned red, like he was about to bleed. He softened his bite before drawing blood..

"I didn't mean to scare you," Crispin said, almost pitifully.

"What did you mean to do then?"

"I meant to torture and kill her."

That deadpan honesty terrified me. I stepped back again, pressing my butt against the bed and staring at Crispin with horror. I continued to wrestle with my feelings for him. I wanted severing my connection to him to be easy but whenever I stood in front of Crispin, I couldn't help but fall into the disturbingly magnetic pull that always sucked me in when he was around.

"Why?" I asked him, stepping closer to him and yielding to feelings I should have done better at suppressing during my time apart from Crispin.

"Because she hurt you."

"No. That's not why," I whispered. I had my suspicions about the darkness inside Crispin, but now I'm sure that there are parts of him so unbearably dark that they scare him. I couldn't help but remember what happened when we first met. He watched all my emotions play out on my face. Crispin was intuitive – especially when it came to me. For the first time, Crispin averted his eyes. I had mixed feelings about finally getting to him successfully.

"There might have been other reasons," he murmured.

Then he added quickly, "I'm not attracted to her. It wasn't... like that."

I understood that part. What I didn't understand was why Crispin enjoyed violence. I wanted to know what the appeal was. I wanted to know if he ever felt those urges about me. If he was serious about those too.

"I don't want to be afraid of the man I love."

He met my gaze again and shrugged.

"Don't be afraid then."

"It's hard… since you jumped out of my closet wielding a knife. Five seconds ago."

The corner of his lips tugged into a sexy, but somewhat evil-looking smile.

"I surrendered it. And I'll surrender to you, Twiggy," he breathed.

I wrapped my arms around my waist. Crispin reached for them and pulled them away.

"Don't cover your stomach," he whispered, touching me slowly. "I miss that stomach."

I wanted to tell him to stop but the lightest touch from Crispin Barclay could melt me into a thousand pieces. He was *mine*. And I still belonged to him. I didn't want to jump into his arms without a second thought to what had happened, but I didn't hate Crispin. I couldn't.

"I missed you too. Ben and Libby were great. But I missed you."

"They're good friends," Crispin agreed. "Vi and Jack are… mental. But they were fine. I wanted to call you."

"I'm glad you didn't."

His arm fell away from me for a moment and he stuffed his hands in his pockets.

"Right."

He seemed like he was going to leave for a moment, but

then he closed the distance between us and put his hand on the small of my back, pulling me against him roughly. All 6'6" of my tall, hunky blond white boy pressed against me and I was completely weak. Crispin was beyond sexy. He was impossible to ignore. It was even worse because I loved him. So I didn't just see his broad chest or his impossibly chiseled stomach... I knew his heart.

"I can't let you go," he whispered.

I wasn't strong enough to say no to Crispin Barclay. I wasn't strong enough to push him away again. I didn't know if I wanted things to be like they were before. The change in what I'd seen in him had been so sudden that I wasn't really *over him*. I just got so scared of what he could do.

I didn't want him to be a killer. I wanted him to be *mine*.

"We should stop. Mandeep could come back at any time."

"I don't care," he growled.

He bent his head to my neck and kissed me softly. His lips were impeccably soft and warm. He trailed kisses along my shoulder as his grasp on me tightened. Crispin's gravitational pull was yanking me away from all common sense. I could feel him reeling me in and my conflicting desires for him cresting like a rogue wave.

"I'd rather not go back to my dorm room without fucking you," he said.

His voice was *perfect*. He sounded like one of my mom's celebrity crushes – *Hugh Grant*. Except Crispin sounded better because his voice was deeper and unlike a celebrity, he was right in front of me where I could feel the warmth of his breath and gaze into his unreasonably gorgeous blue eyes.

"Crispin..." I murmured, trying to stick to my guns and stay away from the man I knew would shatter my heart into a thousand pieces if I let him. Crispin stayed singularly focused on his desires.

"I miss your cunt," he said, running his tongue over his lips. "I can't fall asleep without your cunt on my lips. *I fucking need you.*"

"Can't you just... masturbate?" I asked weakly.

"Why on earth would I want to do that when I could torture myself by imagining you in Glottenham... sleeping in my bed without me. I'm *very* good at delayed gratification."

His hand had fastened in a vice grip around my waist and Crispin's eyes gleamed mischievously. The crotch of his trousers tented out in the biggest hard-on I'd ever seen him have.

"I waited patiently," he whispered.

I couldn't stop myself from reaching out and wrapping my hand on his bulge along the outside of his trousers. Crispin groaned and fell forward against me. My other hand instinctively slid up his shirt as I teased my fingers along his chest and chiseled muscles. His muscles were *so* big. I couldn't even wrap my hand around any of them. Crispin moved his hips slightly, rubbing his crotch against my hand, begging me to acknowledge the intensity of his erection.

"I want you," he breathed into my ear, nibbling on my ear lobes and hoisting me onto my bed. My bed had been elevated enough so that if I sat on it, I was positioned right between Crispin's legs. I could look into his eyes properly now. He still hadn't been sleeping. I wondered what else he'd been up to. Not like this was time to talk. He pushed his crotch against me firmly and grabbed onto a handful of my hair, tilting my neck and kissing it gently before whispering into my ear again, "Let me fuck you, babe."

"Crispin... that's dirty..." I said, struggling to come up with a legitimate reason for pushing him away now that I already let him kiss me. My protest meant nothing. Crispin knew exactly what I liked and he knew he was giving it to me now...

"Good. I like dirty."

He kissed me more ferociously as my fingers tangled in his long hair. I edged my hips forward, grinding them against his hardness. I wanted him inside me now. I didn't want to say no. I never wanted to say no to Crispin Barclay's body. I didn't want him to leave even if Mandeep could walk in at any time. Not like I wanted her to meet me like this... I just couldn't care.

He slipped his hand into my pants and found me wet. He groaned as he pressed his hand between my folds and traveled slowly up to the length of my slit.

"That's good," he whispered.

He took his fingers out and licked them clean before diving back between my legs. He'd moved slowly at first for his pleasure, touching me the way he wanted to and then he pushed a finger inside me and massaged my clit with his other fingers. He kissed me as his hand moved against me, touching the most sensitive parts of me with a tender and slow movement.

"You're soft..." he murmured, kissing my shoulders and pressing his fingers into me deeper. I cried out, leaned forward over Crispin's shoulder, allowing a cascade of curls to drape over his pale back. His fingers moved inside me faster as Crispin used my moans to guide where he touched me. When I bucked my hips forward against him, he clutched my lower back, guiding me and letting me use his hands to cum.

I came three or four times before he pulled his fingers away and stuck his tongue between them, licking me off him. I slipped my pants and underwear off, quivering with desire as Crispin stood between my legs and I sat on my half-made bed.

"Hurry," I whispered.

People were moving around the dorm outside my door. I didn't want anyone to hear us. I grabbed Crispin's butt with my ankles and drew him toward me. I wanted to see that big white dick out of his pants. Sure, I'd missed Crispin's personality but I also missed *this*.

Crispin lowered his trousers and eased his hardness out. It was so easy to forget how *enormous* his dick was. It was my brain's way of coping with the fact that Crispin was so much bigger than a normal guy. His dick could be intimidating it was so big.

I scooted my hips to the edge of the bed. My thighs dripped more as Crispin moved toward me and I felt the warmth of his thighs sliding against mine. Soccer boys have *such* nice thighs. Crispin's were incredible with hard muscle in all the right places and a nice sinewy ass that was perfect to grab onto.

His cheeks flushed as he pressed his forehead to mine. The blushing tip of his dick reflected the fluorescent over-head lights as Crispin edged toward me. He had a condom, thankfully. I can't promise I would have been safe if he hadn't. Crispin made me feel crazy and impulsive sometimes. I guess now was one of those times.

He pressed the tip of his cock against me and I gasped as I

grabbed onto his back and let him slide inside me to the hilt. He wasn't slow or hesitant this time.

"I need you," he growled as he thrust his hips forward and moved his hand slowly to my clit.

I moaned and pushed my hips forward. I didn't want to feel like this. I didn't want to feel like I needed Crispin. I didn't want to feel like I'd forgiven him yet. I still wanted to think. I still needed to consider whether his dark side was just too much for me to handle. But with his enormous body pressed against mine, I couldn't fear anything. All I wanted was *more*. Crispin had that effect on me.

And there was always more of him to have. He withdrew his hips slowly, taking his time to enter me slowly. With our size difference, he had to go slow if he didn't want to hurt me. Which he never did. He pressed the small of my back, pulling me close to him as my legs wrapped around his pale thighs, covered in thick blond hair.

"You feel... so tight..." He whispered into my ear as his hips moved slowly. I grabbed onto Crispin's back and pulled him closer to me. I gasped as his dick filled me up, touching every inch of my walls and his fingers massaged my clit expertly, making me hotter and needier. For a man who didn't have a lot of time, Crispin was making love to me slow. But each thrust was firm and pleasurable. I bucked my hips toward him and he moved his fingers slower, not just touching me but feeling my responses and letting the energy from his fingers pulse between my legs.

"I'm gonna cum," I breathed, bending my head forward and unconsciously sinking my teeth into Crispin's shoulders to stop from moaning as my chest shuddered and one of the best climaxes I'd ever had surged through me. Crispin groaned as I bit down on him and pressed his dick into me deeper. With that last deep thrust, I felt his monstrous dick pulse and empty between my legs.

He grinned as he finished and kissed me without a moment of hesitation.

"I still love you. I might be a monster to everyone else but I'd never hurt you."

My heart did a hopeful little thud. My hope always drew me in. I wanted to believe him. Crispin was so damn gorgeous that he could convince me of anything. I couldn't tell if it was his objective beauty or my attraction to him that made him so compelling.

I nuzzled closer to him.

"I love you," he repeated.

I believe you, I wanted to say. But I said nothing. I just breathed slowly, exhaling against Crispin's large, bare chest as I held him. I didn't want to unravel my legs from his torso. I didn't want to do *anything* that would pull me away from Crispin Barclay.

We both heard more voices in the dorm hallway and knew we had to get dressed. Crispin hurried into his clothes and I dressed quickly. My cheeks flushed. This didn't mean we were back together but... I didn't want to say goodbye to Crispin yet. I just needed time to think.

He raked his fingers through his hair but it wouldn't lie down flat no matter how he tried. He pulled his hoodie up over it, letting the tuft of wild blond hair stick out as he gave up and sank his hands into the hoodie pockets.

"I don't want this to be over. I want... I want to be a good boyfriend."

"I just need more time," I said, my voice sounding hoarse.

"How much?" he asked.

"I don't know," I said, although our plans for Easter break loomed in the back of my mind. We had plans together. "Maybe Easter?"

"Fine," he said, looking at me like it wasn't fine at all. "I'll be looking out for you. So keep eating. Keep seeing your therapist. Okay?"

"Okay. What are you going to do about John?"

"I dunno. Barbados again for Spring Break. You can still come. I want you there."

I bit down on my lower lip and shrugged. He was always so sure of himself and I felt like an insecure mess. I didn't know what to do with that.

"Sure. Yeah. No matter what, we'll at least be friends, right?" I offered.

Crispin gave me a fiercely angry look. But then his face softened and through gritted teeth he said, "Yeah, babe. Friends. I'd love that."

Before I could question how true that was, Mandeep opened the door and walked in. She'd missed us having sex by only a couple minutes.

Mandeep greeted me with instant enthusiasm, "Amina! It's me. Mandeep. New roommate. Hello. New roommate's boy toy... hello. Welcome to the better half of Year 12. Lady Cavendish is *so* excited to have you."

Chapter Four

rispin waved and smiled awkwardly.

"HELLO, MANDEEP."

"Oh, you can call me Mandy. Crispin, I'm sure you'll be here a lot. Thanks for not letting me walk in on you. Now, toodles. It's girl time. Us girls have been talking about Amina on the group chat for *ages*."

So far, this was a far cry from the picture of a field hockey bully Vi Bainbridge painted for me. Crispin awkwardly excused himself after casting me a sidelong glance. Once he was gone, Mandeep grinned.

"You're dating the hottest guy in our whole year and now we live together. I cannot *wait* to ask you questions."

"Yeah, girl. It's been real..."

"Your accent! You *really* have one. Do we have any classes together?"

"I think we had history last semester."

She shrugged and muttered, "Boring. We only talk about how great England was. Not in my opinion. Half-Pakistani, Half-Indian. Not exactly a huge fan of the Empire."

I liked her. At least I thought I liked her. Mandeep was around my height, average sized for a girl with deep cinnamon colored skin and a reddish birthmark across her face under her eyes and cheeks. She wore her hair in a sleek black ponytail and dressed impeccably in a wardrobe of clothing that only had four colors – olive green, black, white and navy blue.

Gold hoop earrings gleamed in the sunlight as she folded her arms and considered me with a curious look.

"So... everyone says all the bitches live in Lady Randalls. Is that why you left?"

"The bitches kicked me out," I said, not realizing how bitter I was until I said it out loud.

Mandy rolled her eyes and said, "I can't imagine. I loathe Ella Novak. She plays field hockey and she's seriously the most annoying person."

I snickered. What the hell would Mandy think if I told her Ella Novak dated my father? Maybe they were back together. My dad had a way of sinking his teeth into his prey and never letting go.

I didn't even know if Ella would be back on campus after the incident with Crispin. He'd nearly killed her so he was just lucky she hadn't run off to tell the police. Wasn't he in enough trouble already without actually trying to kill someone?

"I can tell you hate her," Mandy said. "So we're going to get along swimmingly. Our wallmates are Mary Little and

Theresa Cann. They don't talk to anyone. Across the hall, Julia Anders and Sarah Getty. They're both cool."

Mandy pulled out her phone and apparently texted the dorm group chat because four girls piled into my room, welcoming me into the dorm. Paige Rapetti (great-grand-daughter of the school's founder) and Jane Fitz (her room-mate) walked in first followed by Julia and Sarah G. They all introduced themselves and offered to help me unpack. Because of Sarah Clifford, Sarah always went by Sarah G.

I didn't see why I shouldn't let them help. The girls pulled my boxes open and dutifully assisted my unpacking. I couldn't imagine Katrina doing anything like this. Mandy spilled the beans that I was dating Crispin and the gushing commenced. Half the girls probably already knew, but half of boarding school gossip was pretending that you didn't know the boarding school gossip already. That was how you got the juicy details.

I didn't have the heart to tell Mandy that Crispin and I were in an in-between phase and I wouldn't exactly brag about dating him right now, but I couldn't lie about my Christmas break.

"I saw Vi's castle pics," Sarah G. said, her voice sounding deep and gravely for a skinny blond girl who looked like an Instagram model. "She's so bloody posh."

"I wish I could go to her house," Julia said, adjusting her lip gloss in a hand mirror. "I bet it's so amazing."

The girls all wanted to know what classes I was taking and what time I liked eating breakfast. They didn't like the usual cliques at Rapetti and had 'dorm tables' for anyone in L.C. Who didn't have friends to eat with to have somewhere to eat.

"Misaki leads dorm dinners," Mandy explained. "You don't have to come, but it's fun a couple nights a week."

I froze. Misaki? As in Crispin's older ex-girlfriend who *hated* me? She'd been Daniella's friend and they'd made my life living hell last semester. I bit my lip and muttered, "I didn't know she lived here."

I didn't want my new friends to see how scared that made me.

"She's an *incredible* prefect," Julia said. "Seriously. I talked to her about this guy I shagged last semester who gave me an STD. She was wonderful."

"Stop having sex with gross guys," Paige said, a smirk on her face.

"You have sex!" Julia accused.

"No. I give blowjobs. There's a difference," Paige answered.

The conversation descended into an argument about sex and blowjobs. I realized after a few minutes that Crispin rarely asked me for blowjobs. He never really forced the issue and I never offered. Because of what the girls were saying, I wondered if I'd had it all wrong and they weren't so bad. I'd had it way wrong with my period.

Just when I was going to text Crispin and ask him about blowjobs, Vi and Katrina stopped by. I was looking down at my phone when they pushed the door open and the room fell into a hush. I smiled at Vi and Katrina, but I sensed the other girls in the room were uncomfortable. Vi waved and offered a polite but soft hello. Katrina looked around and nodded at Julia.

"Hey Fat Julia," she said. "Put your dick sucking lips to work over break?"

Julia turned red and then said softly, "Whatever, Katrina."

Katrina snorted and then glanced at me.

"Listen, slut. We're going to get super drunk tonight and I think you'd rather do something cool than hang around here."

Drunk? Wasn't Katrina pregnant? I forgot how good she could be at pretending. I didn't glance up from the books I was pretending to arrange on my desk. The other girls in the room were quiet and waiting for an explosion that we all sensed might happen.

"I'm actually having a good time," I said, not bothering to be polite. I was here, enjoying L.C. With my new friends. Vi hadn't done anything wrong, but she was letting Katrina walk all over her and I wouldn't let my new dorm mates think I was a stupid pushover. I learned my lesson last semester. Hell, I'd learned my lesson over Christmas Break when I had to confront something far scarier than Katrina, desperately hiding her pregnancy beneath multiple hoodies and a pair of sweatpants. I could tell that she was pregnant, but most people looking at her couldn't. Her disguise was solid, I'll give her that.

Katrina didn't know I knew her secret but that didn't matter. I still knew she had to be careful. So what was this talk of getting super drunk anyway? Vi was turning red, so she was probably struggling to keep her thoughts to herself.

Katrina scoffed haughtily, "You're having a good time? It makes sense that you'd fit in with the losers."

Paige Rapetti piped up. "Really, Bible? We're the losers?"

Paige smirked, like she wasn't taking any of this seriously. She probably wasn't. I didn't know Paige well, but she was an established art freak. I didn't mind the art freaks because a lot of them dressed like me, including Paige who liked combat boots and dark liner around her blue eyes.

"Shut up, anorexic," Katrina huffed. "Now, Amina. Hurry. Seriously."

"Katrina, can you chill out?" Vi said, frustration finally cracking through her pleasant demeanor. She flashed me an apologetic look. This time, it wasn't enough. Vi wanted to keep everyone happy.

"You know what? I actually want a break, okay? I'll come find you guys later."

"Amina!" Vi begged. But it was too late. She'd chosen Katrina for the time being and I needed my space. I ushered them out the room and shut the door.

Now the girls were looking at me. Jane Fitz snorted and pretended she wasn't laughing. That rubbed me the wrong way.

Sarah Getty plugged my laptop into the wall, finishing her work setting up my desk and then said in her deep, tomboyish voice, "Are those seriously your friends?"

"Yeah. I mean. We lived together in L.R. It was cool."

Julia rolled her eyes and pouted. Her lips were pretty and covered in a thick layer of clear lip gloss.

Julia explained their little problem out loud, saying, "Katrina's such a bitch to me because August Barclay hit on me at a party. I swear everyone in this dorm thinks I'm lying but they definitely had something."

I bit my lip, trying to keep Katrina's secret. I silenced my phone from Vi's apology text and hung out with the girls in my dorm. They'd helped me set up my room, then they introduced me to everyone except Misaki who would arrive late because of her flight from Japan. We had dinner together as a dorm in the dining hall. I noticed Katrina glancing over at me from her table and then whispering to Vi. Sigh. I didn't expect Violet to stop talking to Katrina but it was like the second we got back to campus, she was under her thumb again.

Whatever. I felt the hairs on the back of my neck stand up and when I glanced over my shoulder, I saw him. He must have been there when I came in, but I didn't notice him untl he started staring at me like I was a juicy cheeseburger.

Crispin sat with Kaito Cammish in the corner of the dining hall and they both stared at me intently. Crispin's staring didn't bother me, but Kaito always made me deeply uneasy. I hoped Crispin wasn't planning anything. Especially not anything evil. Since he was staring, I actually ate something. *Ugh. Annoying.*

By the time dinner ended, Mandeep Desai was still bubbly and excited with stamina for socializing I could never hope to achieve. She got more sullen as we walked back to our room together. When we were alone she got really serious and then said, "Amina? Can I confess something?"

"Yeah. Sure."

"I... I know you're dating Crispin but last semester I... I offered to give him a blowjob. It was embarrassing and he turned me down and I don't fancy him or anything. I just didn't want you to think I was hiding something."

Relief flooded me. I already knew about the blowjob thing but the fact that she told me was so refreshingly... *honest.*

"Thanks. Wow. You totally didn't have to tell me."

"Are you upset?"

"No. Crispin and I are... we get each other. I'm not worried about him."

"Cool. I bet it's so annoying that everyone wants to bang your boyfriend. I'd totally be freaking out."

"Do you have a crush on anyone?" I teased.

Mandeep's birthmark turned a darker shade of copper, even if the rest of her face didn't change. It was the coolest facial mark I'd ever seen, but she tilted her head down when she caught me staring at it. *Ugh, awkward moment, Amina.*

"Yeah. But he'd totally never notice me or anything."

"Who?"

"Did you ever have Doukas?" She asked.

Before I could talk to her about our sexy teacher's thick biceps an envelope slid under our door. We heard footsteps running down the hall as Mandy approached it.

"It's got your name on it," she said, picking it up and wrinkling her brow.

She opened the door and glanced down the hallway.

"I don't see anyone," Mandy said, shutting the door again.

My first assumption was that the envelope was from Crispin. It was a Manila envelope, which made me think of the information we'd uncovered over the holiday. I didn't think it would be anything worse than that. I shrugged and took the envelope from Mandy, peeling it open.

I lost my grasp of the thick paper as soon as I saw what was on the page. I must have made a noise between a gasp and a horrific yelp as I dropped it.

My roommate asked nervously, "What is it?"

Chapter Five

"It's... a print out of..."

"THAT IS A HUGE PENIS!" Mandy shrilled. Then her finger jumped to the text written on the bottom, almost like a horrific social media caption.

I've already planned your rape. No one can protect you now.

"Oh my God!" Mandy screamed, "This is horrific. Amina! We've got to report this."

I didn't just have to report it. This was Crispin's dick pic. The same dick pic that had spread around the school only this time with a rape threat. I told him to take it seriously. And then a troubling thought occurred to me. *I can't even admit it to myself but this could be something... terrible. Maybe Crispin's darkness had grown worse. Maybe he had lost control. Maybe he was behind this.* I'd never questioned him like this before.

"Who would do something like this?" Mandy said, aghast.

My heart pulsed nervously. This time, we wouldn't wait around for something horrible to happen. I didn't want to answer her.

"We should report this," I agreed. "I just need to talk to Crispin first."

Mandy nodded seriously and slipped into her soft leather black flats.

"I'll go ask the other girls if they've seen anything. Don't worry. This sort of stuff doesn't happen in L.C."

I texted Crispin the moment Mandy left the room.

ME: did you slip something under my door
Crispin: no
Crispin: what happened?

I BREATHED A SIGH OF RELIEF. Even if Crispin scared me, I still loved him. I still trusted him and wanted to believe him. I told him what happened. Crispin didn't reply for a few moments.

CRISPIN: I can come over tonight.

I BIT my lower lip hard. I knew what would happen if Crispin came over. I'd curl up into his hoodie and then I'd smell him. Crispin always smelled amazing. He was warm and sexy. If I pushed my butt against him, I'd remember that he had an amazing body and I'd think I could get away with just a *little* touch. By the time that happened, I'd lose control.

. . .

Me: don't come over

Crispin: k

MANDY and I marched over to Dean Leonard's office. Dean Leonard looked stressed when we opened the door. I hadn't seen her since last semester and I expected her to email me about a meeting at least. She glanced up from her computer and took a few moments before plastering on her school administrator's smile.

"Ladies. Please tell me there isn't a problem with your room assignment already."

"No, Dean Leonard," Mandy said respectfully. "Someone's harassing Amina with a picture of a boy's cock."

Well. I wouldn't have put it that way. Dean Leonard glanced at me and raised an eyebrow.

"Well. It certainly is a boy's cock," Dean Leonard said, running her finger over the length of the page. I couldn't confess that I knew whose cock it was. Crispin hadn't written the rape threat. Hadn't Dean Leonard seen this picture before?

Dean Leonard stared at it for a few seconds before catching herself and flipping it over.

"A rather large one…" Mandy muttered.

Dean Leonard cleared her throat and her cheeks turned pick.

"Miss Desai… Thank you, kindly."

"When did you receive this?"

I told her what I knew, but I didn't bother telling either of them that I knew the picture was Crispin's and I wasn't the first person to receive it. Once we'd finished reporting it,

Mandy paused outside of Dean Leonard's office and she gave me a serious look.

"Do you know Jane Fitz?"

"She's a redhead in our dorm. I just met her."

"She knows Ella Novak from secondary. They went to an all-girls boarding school and the bullying was brutal. You should talk to her."

"No offense, Mandy, but Jane scares me."

"Because she's ginger?"

"No. Because she hangs out with Sarah Clifford who called me a slut every day of last semester."

Mandy nodded.

"Yeah. Sarah's intense... Both of them are. But Jane will talk to you about Ella. She hates Ella. Trust me."

"What does Ella have to do with anything?"

"Talk to Jane. I just don't feel comfortable talking about her past."

"Cool. Want to grab a bite?" I asked. I was hungry again.

Mandy agreed and she began excitedly telling me about her grandparents' house in Mumbai. When we sat together at dinner, I didn't expect anyone to join us. It was quiet, with very few people indulging in a dinner this late. Mandy was happy to eat and to chat, but there were only a couple other occupied tables, mostly with athletes and loners. Three guys on the rugby team ate together and I didn't recognize most of the loners.

Mandy and I weren't part of a special clique, just room-mates eating together. When Vi and Sarah Clifford entered the dining hall, my back stiffened and I glanced up at them nervously.

Mandy was asking me curious questions about Barbados

and didn't notice how distracted I was. Vi and Sarah made a beeline for our table and they looked serious.

"May we sit here please?" Sarah asked politely.

I hadn't seen her since the incident with my dad when she and Violet had helped me escape. No one had mentioned that to my face (thank goodness) and Ella's attempts to spread the word around campus obviously hadn't worked. That might have been because of Crispin. My heart did a backflip-fail just thinking about him. Mandy encouraged Sarah and Violet to sit. She was friendly, but a little awkward around them. Vi tried her best at small talk, but Sarah couldn't stop herself from interrupting.

"We would like to humbly request your help. Mandy, you can help too."

"Me? Help with what?"

Vi said proudly, "We're doing a campaign to raise awareness of sexual assault."

Mandy wrinkled her nose.

"Okay… Will anyone at this bloody school care?"

Sarah glanced at me in a gesture that I realized was meant to be supportive and then she said seriously, "We'll make them care. It's about time we all have a wake up call. Rape happens."

"Is that your slogan?" Mandy asked skeptically.

Vi hurriedly interjected with, "Well, we're workshopping. We were thinking… Stop All Sexual Assault might work."

"Hard to argue with that," Mandy said.

I explained to her that I'd told Vi about the dick pic. Then we all told stories about how we'd been treated inappropriately on campus. I wasn't the only person Felix Stubbins had rudely groped. I shared that fate with Mandy. We'd all experienced comments, groping, harassment… and I hadn't even spilled all the details about the horrible spanking the football boys forced me to endure when I was new.

"It stops here," Vi said definitively.

"What about that? That could be a slogan," Mandy said.

Sarah nodded. She didn't seem nervous around Mandy. I'd have to press Vi about her rumors.

"Ladies…"

We all glanced up. I didn't need to look up to tell who it was from the enormous shadow. Few boys loomed over you the way Crispin Barclay did. He looked like he hadn't been sleeping again and he barely looked at me, even if he'd obviously approached our table to talk to me. Without asking and without waiting, he pulled up a chair and sat between me and Mandy.

He leaned over and took some of Mandy's hair from her ponytail, pressing it to his nose.

"Your shampoo smells incredible."

Crispin glanced over at me to see if I was jealous, probably. *Boy, bye!* Mandy glanced at me nervously and then muttered something about a brand at an Indian shop. I couldn't let Crispin's little interruption continue. *Hello, white boy, we're talking about sexual assault. It's girl talk.*

"Crispin? We're a little busy here," I snapped.

"I can tell. Girls conspiring makes me nervous."

Sarah stared at Crispin, her cheeks reddening. She was either nervous around him or she still liked him. That made me ten times more jealous than Crispin smelling Mandy's hair. He'd been with Sarah. He liked Sarah in the past. Now that I'd dumped him, maybe he'd start liking her again. I knew we were just on a break, but I didn't know how Crispin saw it. Maybe he was pulling away from me. Insecurities welled in my chest, even if I didn't want them to. *He's bad for me. I shouldn't lean into this addictive pull towards him.*

"We're planning a sexual assault awareness campaign," Sarah said without blushing or gushing.

Vi nodded agreeably now someone else had blurted out the awkward part.

"Amina and Mandy are helping us. We're turning this campus feminist."

"I see. Are you going to cancel football, then?"

"Just because we're feminists doesn't mean we hate sports," Vi snapped.

"Right," Crispin muttered awkwardly.

Then he sat up and his face got bright.

"Perhaps I could help. Couldn't you use a boy to raise awareness?"

"A boy's the one who harrassed Amina," Mandy muttered.

"What happened to Amina?" Crispin said. He seemed genuinely clueless, even if I'd just explained it to him. *Good acting, I guess.*

Mandy explained. I knew she was just trying to help, but I didn't want Crispin to go all crazy on me. I had no choice but to show him the picture. Crispin didn't blink or blush. We both obviously knew it was his dick. Sarah Clifford probably knew. But they were English. They didn't acknowledge it. Mandy might have been the only one who didn't know exactly whose cock we were staring at. Crispin hurriedly folded the picture in half.

He sounded disgusted as he huffed, "A rape threat? Is that really what men have descended to?"

"Yes," I said, my heart fluttering nervously. "That's why we don't need a man's help."

"Who gave this to you, Amina?" He asked. I glared at him and elbowed him in the chest. We already discussed this. He was a little too committed to the bit and I suspected it was just because he wanted to get involved in my life and get close to me.

"I don't know, Crispin. Do you?" I grumbled. He was the only boy at the table and honestly, I wanted him to go away.

Three-quarters of the table stared at him nervously while Mandy obliviously heaped cumin powder from her handbag onto her cubes of tofu.

"No," Crispin said. "But I'll find out. I've been in an investigative mood. If the ladies will allow it, I'd like to help."

Chapter Six

I couldn't chase Crispin off without agreeing to let him help us. Then Mandy and Vi gushed about how sweet he was. Sarah politely declined from commenting which was probably most comfortable for both of us. She hadn't exactly spoken to me about last semester, but I appreciated the fact that she wasn't calling me a slut under her breath every five minutes.

We planned for a while together and Vi agreed to ask Dean Leonard for permission to make everything unfold the way we'd wanted. If we could get something planned for the end of the semester, we'd be poised to make changes for our ascent to Year 13. The glorious Year 13…

I wasn't the best artist, but I was better than anyone else at the table, so my assignment was making some designs for our campaign. Mandy went to study at the library with Paige Rapetti and Sarah G.

I wanted to work quietly in our dorm room so I declined joining them.

Studying worked for a while to distract me from my

whirling thoughts. Then I encountered a question on my homework assignment about the black Tudors in England and one research tab later, I was staring at my desk drawer and considering the papers inside it. With Crispin, Ben and Libby, I'd pretended to be all cool about knowing the identity of my birth parents but I'd kept a big secret from all of them too.

I couldn't stop thinking about my birth parents. That was the secret. I couldn't stop thinking about the money and the fact that they'd left me to suffer at the hands of John Hewett and Frances. My mother was in England somewhere, probably waiting for her chance to swoop in and ruin my life. Again.

I opened the folder Ben and Libby had given to me. Instead of studying Keats and Chaucer, I studied the documents. I re-read everything twice. I could only bring myself to look at this stuff when I was alone.

Christy & Elijah Richard. I wondered what they were like. I'd resisted the urge to Google them until now. My therapist wanted me to take things slow. I'd just started getting comfortable eating three meals a day. She didn't know about the break up with Crispin yet and she definitely didn't know how close I was to a fateful Google search. We only had one session since I had been back at school and it had been predictable. *Sigh.*

I started my research with Elijah Richard. The first page I turned up showed both of my parents. I clicked on their website and stared at the banner image — a couple embracing each other. A black couple. A happy black couple. My stomach tightened again.

Tasty Creole Kitchen. My birth parents owned a catering

company. My stomach tightened. There were two kids in the picture with them. Kids who looked like me. All the emotions I'd tried so hard not to feel around Crispin Barclay came out when I was alone. They had other kids. They'd sold me for a fast buck and forgotten all about me. How the hell could I have ever believed they cared?

I clicked off the page and shoved the folder in my desk drawer. I couldn't handle this. I thought I was strong enough, but I wasn't. And I was so done with being alone. I wanted Crispin to stop scaring the crap out of me and I wanted to feel better about getting back together with him but more than that... I wanted Crispin.

I messaged him and waited a few minutes and he didn't message back.

ME: Finally done with homework tonight. Did you get everything done?

BEFORE I COULD GET all mad and text him again, Mandy came back into the room with a midnight snack for me. English kids were obsessed with "midnight feasts" – a concept I did not agree with or understand. Mandy's midnight feast was better than I expected, so I perked up a little, despite the vast amount of food I already consumed today.

She hadn't brought me a shitty little apple or anything. She made me a *really* nice sandwich. It was tasty. She sat on her bed with a happy look on her face.

"Everyone says I make the best sandwiches. I'm glad you

like it," Mandy said, her eyes glimmering with pleasure at my expressions of gratitude.

That shit slapped! She'd used pepperoni, pesto and barbecue sauce alone with turkey breast and ciabatta bread. That sandwich was *luxurious*.

"So..." Mandy said. "Is Crispin coming over tonight?"

My mouth was full of sandwich so I mumbled through it, "What do you mean?"

"I didn't have a proper roommate last semester but he's your boyfriend and he's really fit. I assume you're shagging him?"

"Well. Yeah. But... I can go over to his room."

I'd rather chew Crispin out in front of annoying ass Devin than let my roommate know what a mess I was too soon. Mandy was very relaxed about the whole thing.

"Cool," she said. "If you want to have him over, I can sleep on the floor in Sarah G.'s room. She has her workout stuff everywhere, but I just my comforter on the floor."

"I couldn't make you sleep on the floor."

"Trust me, if I was sleeping with a guy that hot, I wouldn't care."

Mandy giggled and I couldn't help but laugh at her infectious bubbly personality. She was a far cry from Katrina. I went to dorm check-in with my roommate and tried to pretend like Misaki ignoring my existence didn't bother me. I didn't think she wanted me in her dorm but I was just glad that she wasn't out right bullying me.

Mandy fell asleep quickly once we got back to our room. She had a little sleep mask on and earplugs, so she didn't mind if I was awake. I worked on our posters for the sexual assault awareness campaign for a bit. By 11 p.m., Crispin still hadn't messaged me back. I wasn't *trying* to be thirsty, but wasn't he the one who always talked about getting back together?

I was finally ready to talk. Maybe even talk about that specifically. I couldn't sneak out of L.C. The same way I snuck out of L.R. It took planning and a bit of work. There was a little platform outside the bathroom closest to our room that I could jump onto. If I hugged the back walls, I could make it to the boys' dormitory without any of the campus security stalking me. Since all the incidents last semester, we had more campus security, something Dean Leonard reminded us of when we'd reported the dick pic and rape threat.

Reporting it had made me less worried, although perhaps I ought to have been worried. I knew Crispin wouldn't let anything happen to me. For all the horror I felt at his lack of remorse with Ella… I hated to admit that his crazy behavior made me feel protected. He really wouldn't let anyone mess with me.

Few other people were awake that late and no one was using the bathroom, so I jiggled the window open and jumped out. Once on the little platform, I used the old fire escape from before the building had been renovated to jump onto the ground. I pressed my back against the wall, suddenly remembering that England in mid-January was freezing. I had a thin black oversized sweater on with a tank top underneath, tight yoga pants and fuzzy boots. Maybe Crispin would let me slide under the covers with him tonight and I could get warm.

My desires for him were wrong, and I knew it, but I told myself that if there wasn't any daylight out, I could hide from the truth of what it meant to want him that badly knowing he was a walking red flag. *I just need him.*

I'd tried to fight it, but I couldn't stay away from Crispin. My heart jumped into my throat as I acted on my urges to be close to him.

I hurried across campus as quickly as I could. Sneaking out again felt dangerous, but I couldn't stop myself from wanting to see Crispin. I found his window easily. At first I thought I might not remember which window belonged to him, but I remembered where he lived quite well. He'd pulled his window shade down, but I could still get to the window.

Crispin never latched windows. Men who are 6'6" don't worry about things like people coming in through the window and threatening their lives. What bliss. I pushed against the window, making a private pledge to build more muscle so jiggling a window open wouldn't be this hard. I heard footsteps inside the room and then Crispin muttered, "I don't hear anything. I'll look."

One of my legs was already through his window when he pulled back the shade.

"Amina!"

He seemed genuinely surprised. But not more surprised than me. There was a very pretty girl sitting on Crispin's bed and she stared at me as my body awkwardly spilled through the window and I landed on Crispin's floor with a humiliating thud.

53

Chapter Seven

In an awkward tangled mess, I tried to get to my feet and recover my dignity. It wasn't going well.

"Really? You're already banging another girl!?" I yelled.

Crispin tried to help me to my feet. I pushed him as hard as I could. I think he actually stumbled backwards. The girl on his bed stared at me bewildered. Crispin began stammering something, but I interrupted him. No way. I'd already survived watching him hook up with Ella Novak and strut out of public restrooms with Sarah Clifford. How many girls could a guy who was "bad with girls" keep hanging around?

"Don't even say anything. We break up for one week and you're already moving on?"

"It's not what you think and don't *push*."

"I can push you if I want to, white boy."

"Amina, seriously. Calm down and I'll explain."

The girl on the bed spoke up finally and said, "Who the bloody hell is that?"

She sounded more bored than outraged. She didn't even go to this school!

"Explain what? You ignore me all day to go pick up some goth townie to ravish in your bedroom!"

The girl giggled.

"I'm *not* ravishing her. I'm not ravishing anyone. Can you calm down, Amina?"

"Don't tell me to calm down!"

I swung at him, but Crispin caught my arm effortlessly and pushed me back against the window, pressing my arm against me. He was firm, but not cruel. Adam's apple bobbed and then he released me from his grasp once he was sure I wasn't going to bolt.

He said sharply, "That's my twin sister. Freddie. This is Amina."

I froze as he said it, examining her with a startled gaze as Crispin's words hit me like a snowball to the head.

Her short black hair was cut into a bob nearly like Vi Bainbridge's but blunter. And Freddie had bangs. As she gazed up at me from beneath them, I saw that she had her brother's intense fixed gaze, although an utterly different pair of eyes. Crispin and Theo had similar eyes. Very blue and wide. Gorgeous. Even in the dimly lit room, which thankfully, Devin wasn't in, I could tell Freddie's eyes were more of an olive color like algae in a lake.

I wrapped my arms nervously around my waist as I took her all in and realized that I'd made an utter fool of myself. Not only had I come flailing through the window like a desperate stick bug, but now I was gawking at her. I didn't mean to be rude, but the first thought that flashed through my head was that she didn't look like a crazy person.

"Ravishing?" Freddie teased. "Is that what you do to your girlfriends?"

"Shut up, Freddie..." Crispin muttered. He hadn't stopped looking at me. Freddie didn't shut up.

"Who's Amina? You never told me about an Amina in your letters?"

I knew she had been hospitalized for mental health reasons, but Crispin hadn't elaborated. I wondered why he hadn't told her about me...

Crispin glared at her again and I could feel all the anger that I'd just let go of rising again. He hadn't told his twin sister about me? I opened my mouth to say something — probably something impulsive that would turn into a massive argument and possibly get us both in trouble.

"I didn't see your message, babe," he said to me.

Freddie looked taken aback, like it had been more likely to her that I was just a crazed hook-up gone wrong than someone who genuinely meant something to Crispin.

"What's going on?"

He said firmly, "I'm taking her to the cottage. You and I need to talk."

"I can see that."

Freddie chimed in again, "Does Gran know your girlfriend is... you know..."

"She's *not* my girlfriend," Crispin said (and honestly it hurt a little). "She dumped me."

That part. Yeah, that part was my fault. Well, I couldn't exactly un-dump Crispin this instant.

"Right..." Freddie said, her voice sounding chilling in its similar cadence to Crispin's. I didn't know why I expected them to look more alike than they did. Fraternal twins are just siblings who shared a womb.

"What do we need to talk about and I thought... no offense... I thought she was... *locked up.*"

Freddie grinned. "I like her. Wish I could have been at that Christmas dinner."

"I'm sure you do," Crispin muttered.

He reached into my pocket and handed me his car keys. I'd never been in the new car Theo had given him. I assumed he'd already taken other girls on long countryside drives listening to music. But when he closed his palm around my hand, it occurred to me that maybe Crispin couldn't love anyone else the way I couldn't think of anyone else but him.

I glanced up at him, waiting for some instruction. I didn't want to drive his expensive car around and I didn't know anywhere to go. Plus, I had class at 9 a.m. This wasn't how I pictured my night going down.

"Wait for us in the car. I need a few things and I need to get Freddie out of here. If you want to come, I'll take you to the cottage. I didn't want you involved but... I can't say no to you. Ever."

The last word seemed to hurt him and he turned away toward his sister.

"Do you love her?" Freddie asked him. She looked at me again, examining me with wide eyes. "She's really pretty. Not really *my* type but... cute."

"Shut. Up," Crispin snarled at her. He blew wisps of his hair out of his face and touched my cheek.

"Go..." he whispered. "I'll see you at the car?"

"Same place?" I asked softly.

He gave me a gentle nod and then I climbed back out the

57

window. I didn't know what I was doing, but I had Crispin's car keys and I was already sneaking out. I remembered the way to his spot. His new car was *really* nice. I unlocked it and climbed into the back seat. It felt wrong to make Crispin's twin sister sit in the back. The car smelled as new as it was. Crispin had a picture of me tucked into his vent. My heart fluttered when I saw it.

I'd forgotten he'd taken it at Glottenham. I sat in the window and he said the light made my skin look beautiful. I bit down on my lower lip to stop from crying. How could someone who was so sweet have such terrible darkness lurking beneath the surface?

Crispin and his twin sister appeared a few minutes later. I could tell Crispin was yelling when I saw them approaching in the rear view mirror.

By the time they approached the car, Crispin was visibly pissed off, but they'd ceased screaming.

"Why are you in the back?"

"Leave her alone," Freddie said, putting her feet up on the dashboard. "I like the front seat. Better to play our driving games."

"*Our* driving games nearly got us killed in Dubai…"

"Only because you're a shitty driver." Freddie glanced over her shoulder at me, bemused. "Has he nearly killed you with his horrible driving yet?"

Crispin started the car. His large hands cupped around the gear shift tensed angrily. Veins wrapped around his muscular forearms and one bulged out of his neck. Crispin always said he wasn't close with his sister. It was clear she pissed him off, but he seemed protective of her. The last time I'd seen

Crispin that protective had been the night with Ella. The night I'd dumped him.

I knew the drive to the cottage well. As the car sped down the roads, I stared out the window wistfully. Crispin didn't seem in a chatty mood. Freddie teased him after a few moments of tapping her finger along to the rock music she'd turned up on the radio.

"Have you brought *her* to the cottage?"

Crispin's jaw clenched.

"Yes."

"Seriously?"

"I've brought plenty of girls to the cottage that I haven't told you about," he snapped at Freddie.

"Anyone I might like?"

"Stop it," Crispin snarled at her. "Just stop it."

Freddie glanced back at me.

"I apologize for my brother's rudeness. Did you remember Mum's birthday?"

"Of course I remembered."

"You should have visited."

"Why? So you could subject me to this?"

We were all quiet until the cottage. Freddie got out of the car, humming the theme from *Kill Bill*, more to keep Crispin on edge than anything else. Once we were standing, she examined me.

"You look a lot better now that you're not climbing through his window," she said, towering over me.

I'd seriously never seen a girl that tall. Or thin. She was like me before my treatment. Freddie's cheeks were slightly sunken in, but she had high, pretty cheekbones. She was so thin, I could put my hands around her waist. Crispin never mentioned why she'd been hospitalized. He also hadn't mentioned that she was now free. Freddie smiled as she sized me up.

"Nice boots."

"Thanks," I said.

"You're skinny. Crispin always liked super thin girls. Careful you don't gain any weight."

Crispin pinched Freddie's arm so hard, I thought she would yelp. She only winced and yanked her arm away.

"Trying to help."

"You're not helping. You never bloody help," Crispin snarled.

She whined, "Can't you forgive me?"

"I want to," he said.

Once inside, Freddie excused herself to the shower. She'd pulled a small navy blue duffel bag out of Crispin's trunk. Once in the house, he stuck a cigarette between his lips and put on the kettle. Like every stressed Englishman in existence, he believed in the power of a good cup of tea. He leaned against the counter, puffing furiously at his cigarette while he waited for the tea to boil. I didn't say anything for a few moments. Then I leaned against the counter next to him, reminded painfully of how small I was compared to Crispin Barclay.

"I broke her out," Crispin said. "I might have done a terrible, stupid thing. But I had to. Something in those letters… damn it, Amina. I wish you hadn't come tonight."

When did he have time for all of that? I scowled.

"Okay. Thanks."

"I didn't mean that…

"Whatever, Crispin. Keep your secrets. Just take me back to campus."

I had asked for these problems by leaping through Crispin's window in the middle of the night, but that didn't make me any less frustrated by his rejection. What the hell was he doing?

His face softened slightly. "For selfish reasons, I wish you could stay. Trust me.. But I want to protect you and now that you're here... I can't."

"What's going on?" I asked, wanting to pinch him until he told me the entire truth about why he broke Freddie out and what he was doing.

"You'll regret knowing all my secrets," he said with a tightening voice.

"I won't."

Crispin scoffed.

"Haven't you forgotten that you dumped me? You don't even know the darkest parts of my life and it's too much. I get it. I'm too much for you to handle."

I wanted to tell him that it wasn't true. That I *could* love him. I just wanted him to stop hurting people. I wanted him not to think of violence and darkness. But how could he stop? Like me, Crispin had been through hell. I knew more than anyone how it could change someone. I reached for his hand and Crispin eagerly snuggled his fingers against mine.

"If I tell you what I've been hiding... why I can't sleep... you'll never forgive me, Twiggy. And I couldn't ask you to forgive me."

"I just want the truth. I've been lied to my entire life. All I want is the truth," I whispered to him. Crispin's face darkened. I didn't know if the truth would make me want to stay with him, but I couldn't stop myself from running headfirst towards Crispin Barclay's darkness.

Chapter Eight

I was numb after he explained how everything connected. He spent the rest of the drive telling the story slowly, unraveling his secrets like a horrifying present. I sat there numb in the driver's seat of his car, unable to pay attention to the music Crispin played.

It was all connected. Crispin's parents murders'. Freddie's institutionalization. August's death. And her…

He parked the car outside the cottage. I hadn't asked where we were going, but the familiarity of the drive likely hadn't prompted me to. I couldn't bring myself to move yet from the driver's seat. Crispin's secrets imprisoned me in place.

"There's someone else at the cottage," Crispin whispered. "But I don't want you to freak out that she's here."

"At this point, I expect you to keep a girl in your back pocket for when I'm not around," I muttered bitterly. "Do you have one in the glove compartment too?"

Crispin put his cigarette out on the handy Barbados souvenir ashtray.

"Not true," he said. "I can't stop thinking about you. I'm not over you."

"I'm not over you either," I muttered.

"Is that why you came?"

I squirmed uncomfortably.

"Yes."

Crispin sighed as we heard footsteps shuffling out of one of the bedrooms. My chest tightened when Katrina Grigsby came around the corner, dressed in her pajamas and carrying a Bible under her arm. She glowered at Crispin, not even paying attention to me.

"You told her?" Katrina snapped.

"Yes. I love her. I tell her everything."

"That explains why Bainbridge has been acting like such a freak," Katrina groaned, sitting at the little kitchen table and helping herself to a cup of tea. She grumbled something under her breath as she poured the tea.

"Freddie's here," Crispin told her.

Crispin didn't even seem to care that I'd spilled the beans to Vi.

"Good," Katrina said. "Finally. You're *such* a wanker."

Now I really wanted to know what the hell was going on. Katrina glanced at me.

"So. Now that you know I'm a hypocrite, why don't you get it out," Katrina said. "Say all the nasty things you want to say. Call me a slut."

"I don't want to attack you."

"I know I've been a bitch," she said. "I know I was a shitty roommate and I called you a slut. It's just… I'm not really a good person."

She shrugged, as if she'd given up on morality entirely. If

Katrina thought I was going to argue with that statement, she was wrong. Crispin moved his hips closer to mine and reached for another cigarette.

"Give me one," Katrina said, rudely grabbing one from him. Crispin didn't react to her. He seemed completely disinterested.

But if he was so disinterested in Katrina, why on earth was she at his grandparents' cottage? I didn't know if it was just because of August or if there was something more. She took the cigarette and then Crispin reacted. He squeezed her wrist until her hand open and she dropped it. Katrina yelped.

"Smoke and drink while you're pregnant one more time and you'll regret it."

"See what I mean?" she snarled. "Wanker."

"Katrina, stop," I snapped. "You know doing that stuff isn't good for babies. You might be a bad person but you're not that bad."

"I keep thinking being Christian will make me better," Katrina muttered. "It just doesn't work."

She shrugged and set her Bible on the table. She leaned over and groaned.

"You're going to tell her everything aren't you?" She said to Crispin.

Crispin nodded. His hair was getting so much longer and it was so yellow.

"Why? I thought you loved her," Katrina said, snorting as if she didn't believe in love.

"How much do you people talk exactly?" I snapped.

Katrina grinned and teased, "Jealous?"

"No. I'm not jealous. Why would I be jealous of someone pregnant?"

"I deserved that," she said, her smile falling away a bit.

"We talk as much as we need to," Crispin muttered, glowering at Katrina. "More often than I'd like."

"Get over yourself. This is just as much your fault as mine."

Crispin ran his hands over his jaw and a sudden horrific thought occurred to me. That there were even more secrets than I originally thought.

"Wait… is Katrina carrying your baby?"

"No!" Crispin yelled. "Seriously, Amina? That's disgusting. It's August's. Definitely August's"

"Wow, thanks…" Katrina muttered.

Crispin didn't pay her any mind. He turned to me fiercely and grabbed my cheeks.

"I've meant every word of what I said to you. I love you. I love you more than anything. Please… I could never look at another girl the way I look at you."

Katrina made a gagging noise.

"Seriously? This is the type of stuff he says?"

"Shut up," Crispin whispered. He kissed me firmly on the lips and I didn't stop him. His soft rosebud lips parted mine and he pushed me against the counter in an instant of urgency, pulling away when he realized that the instinct to do so had overwhelmed his sense. His cheeks were flushed as he pulled away.

Before Katrina could make another snappy comment, Freddie emerged. She glanced at Katrina and rolled her eyes.

"Katrina."

"Freddie."

I couldn't have begun to guess how all these people were connected and what exactly we were doing here together.

Crispin was on his third cigarette by the time Freddie toweled her hair dry and poured her own cup of tea. Crispin was working his way up to telling me. I could tell.

"It was my idea to frame Daniella," Crispin said. "But she didn't kill my brother."

You could have heard the beating of a moth's wings a mile away, it was so quiet. Before anyone spoke, ringing started in my ears. Ringing that came with hunger. Ringing that came before fainting. Ringing that came before puking all over my boyfriend because he just confessed to me that he framed someone for murder. I suppressed the urge to throw up, quieting the ringing before it was too late.

"Danny's not a nice girl," Freddie finally said.

I was so stunned that I was mentally regressing.

"What do you mean you *framed* Daniella?"

"She's not exactly a sympathetic character," Freddie muttered.

I couldn't argue with that. But Crispin had lied... Again! I needed to hear him tell me why. I needed to hear the truth.

"How the hell can I ever expect to get the truth from you?" I said, pulling away from him. My voice sounded angry, but I just felt sad and betrayed again. We promised no more lies. We promised.

Crispin noticed me moving away from him.

"Don't hear it from me," he huffed.

"I killed August," Katrina said. "But it was an accident. Mostly."

"And... you were stupid enough to do it in front of Daniella," Freddie muttered, tapping her fingers along the side of the cup in a distinct pattern.

"He was playing with both of us. And he knew... he knew

what happened to us both," Katrina said with a twinge of remorse in her voice.

"August got what was coming to him," Crispin said, glaring. I knew he found out afterwards, but it still shook me to my core to hear him say that, especially after how he reacted the night I found August's body.

The hairs on the back of my neck stood up. Just when I wanted to get back together with Crispin, he reminded me that he could be worse than cold-hearted. It was like his very blood was as cold as his eyes. He shifted his hips closer to mine again. Mercifully, he didn't reach for another cigarette.

"So that's it. My roommate's a murderer and my boyfriend's a liar."

My stomach churned with the weight of the secret. How could Katrina do something like this? How could this be real? I played over the events of the past couple months in my head and couldn't believe she had kept a straight face through it all, only shedding a few tears that made her seem realistically depressed.

"Boyfriend?" Crispin said hopefully. I shot him a glare.

"You don't understand what August did to me," Katrina whispered. "I really loved him. He lied about everything. He promised me…"

"Katrina's known our family for years," Crispin said.

"I've never been a fan of her myself," Freddie whispered to me, although obviously Katrina could hear her.

Crispin noticed that Katrina was now too distressed to speak. Her breathing and anxious gasping sounded like she was having a panic attack. Freddie glanced at her unsympathetically. She had a numb expression about all of this, I noticed. Crispin sighed and continued on Katrina's behalf.

"August forced himself on Katrina after promising her he'd wait until dumping Danny to have sex. She found out she was pregnant before Halloween. When my brother found out, he started choking her. I saw that part. I distracted him. Not on purpose. I just didn't know what he was doing. Daniella must have been across the way because I didn't see her. She saw me. Then Katrina…"

"I can tell her," Katrina interrupted, wiping her nose.

"I picked up a rock and I smashed him on the head. Hard."

"Ouch," Freddie whispered, tapping her fingers in the same pattern as before, only much slower. She took a sip of tea and then tucked some of her black hair behind her ears. She was smiling unabashedly. Crispin pretended not to notice and continued telling the story.

He said, "Daniella ran. I tried to chase her but Katrina stopped me. My brother was lying there, immobile… and she tells me she's pregnant and how he did it and I thought of Freddie. And what she'd told me. He made me believe she was a liar. Everyone made me believe she was a liar."

"I've been diagnosed as a nymphomaniac lesbian," Freddie said calmly, with all the enthusiasm one might use to read a newspaper horoscope. "It's only half true. Well. I'm not a lesbian. But I shagged one of my psychiatrists. Nice tits. Fucked up childhood. Therapist and I couldn't fix each other."

Freddie giggled awkwardly and then stopped tapping. Her eyes were wide and she glanced at her brother nervously. She set down her tea and stirred in a lump of sugar. Crispin didn't meet her eyes. He folded his arms and leaned against the counter. He was mumbling now. A little embarrassed.

"She's always been a little… different. I mean… I just believed the diagnosis. But when Katrina explained what he'd done to her," Crispin said, pausing to rake his fingers through his hair. "I began to wonder what else my brother might be capable of. I knew he forced Amina to kiss him. It was so easy for him. I just thought he wanted to piss me off. I just thought Freddie was a liar. She's still a liar."

Then, his twin sister interrupted.

"Everyone thought I was a liar," said Freddie. "And I'm not. Not really."

Crispin pushed his hair out of his face. I noticed he couldn't meet my eyes and then he said, "I didn't want to believe it."

Katrina wiped her nose more carefully this time and appeared to be collecting her composure. I was confused again.

"August *raped* me," Freddie said. "He's been *raping* me. He got me pregnant twice. I've had two abortions for him. Thanks, *Daddy*…"

It was dangerously quiet again. I knew sometimes you just had to spit your trauma out there but what Freddie was saying was… Horrific. I understood what she felt. I hated that we had that common ground, but it felt strangely comforting too.

"I didn't think people did that in families," Crispin said. "Not ours. Not anyone else's."

I bristled nervously. Crispin hadn't wanted to believe me. Few people did when I told them about my dad. But he hadn't had much of a choice when he found me at John Hewett's mercy in a hotel room. He'd fought for me. And then, he'd come around to believing his sister. I felt uncomfortable and nauseous again, and suddenly endeared to Freddie despite her strange behavior. She'd lived in an asylum. Maybe she was just traumatized.

Her next words broke me, because I knew exactly what it was like to be in her position.

"It's worse than that," Freddie said. "It's that no one believes me. Ever. I told him about John Braithwaite four years ago. For God's sake, you moron, he has your eyes."

Freddie's hands trembled slightly and she set down her tea, silently trying to calm herself. Crispin glanced at his feet guiltily.

"I tested John's hair. You were right. He's family," Crispin said.

"Told you so…" Freddie said.

"So you knew?" I blurted out.

I wasn't sure if I liked Freddie or if she scared the crap out of me. She nodded and her face got all sad again. She was like Crispin. A little tough but a little soft too. I felt bad for insinuating that Crispin was going to ravish her now. Ugh, talk about putting my foot in my mouth.

Crispin continued pushing forward, "What he did to Katrina he did nearly exactly to you. The manipulation. The pushing. The… physical act."

Crispin sounded repulsed. I couldn't blame him.

"August had his kinks," Freddie whispered. This time, her voice was angry. Then, Crispin said something that made my blood run cold.

"And so did our dad."

He'd never said a negative word about his parents. When we lay together at night, he'd tell me about his mother's singing. I knew from his grandparents that his family probably hadn't been perfect, but he'd never suggested anything even remotely like this. I didn't even understand exactly what he was suggesting. But it scared me.

"So did Granddad," Freddie whispered.

Crispin's shoulders tensed.

"You weren't lying about him either..." Crispin said. "John's mum was fourteen at conception, fifteen when she had him."

"Who would believe a slut like me?" Freddie said bitterly. "That's what men do. They use you. They abuse you. And then they have the gall to call you a slut so no one ever listens to you. At least my twin brother was decent enough not to have a go at me. So you don't have to worry about him."

"Stop being so self-pitying and get to the point," Katrina snapped. "All of us were abused at some point. It's just life. God's plan."

"Say one word about God's plan and I'll rip August's demon seed out of you with a pair of pliers..." Freddie whispered into her tea.

Definitely Crispin's twin.

Chapter Nine

Freddie up now and her voice was clear and confident. She did what I had to do when I told difficult stories about my life. I had to make it a story in the first place. I had to almost pretend that it happened to someone else. It was too painful to admit that it had happened to me.

"When August was 16, my father and grandfather introduced him to the family tradition. The annual trips to the Pink Plantation. The young girls. The American businessmen. The English businessmen. It's a sick fun house for rich freaks."

Crispin clenched the kitchen counter so tightly, his knuckles turned white. I wanted to reach out and touch him, to tell him that he didn't have to let his anger consume him. Freddie's story held me rapt.

She spooned more sugar into her second cup of tea and continued, "Gran knows about the sex parties... but she doesn't care. She doesn't care that her husband's a nonce. She doesn't care that Mum was so badly abused by him that she married a man twice her age," Freddie said. "The only people worse than the Hargreaves are the Barclays."

My fingers were numb. Crispin's brows pinched together furiously and I could tell from the look on his face that he wanted another smoke. Probably even a drink. This was emotional stuff and Crispin didn't do emotions like this. He didn't enjoy flaying his pain for all to see. Especially not for me to see.

He didn't want to tell me this because he knew what had happened to me and he knew how it would hurt me to hear that his sister had gone through something like what I'd done and he'd done nothing. I didn't know how long he'd known about Freddie, but I didn't think it was very long or Crispin might have tried to kill August himself.

"August was a monster," Freddie whispered. "All the men in my family are monsters."

I could almost detach myself from what was happening around me, but I had been so damn curious about Crispin for so long.

"Don't..." Crispin snarled. "Don't you dare compare me to them."

Freddie ignored him.

"I'm not a liar. And if you won't spit it out, I will. We were all together the night my parents died. I drugged Crispin."

That news hit me like a freight train. I could feel my instincts to withdraw rising in my chest, but my desire to know the truth was stronger.

"I need you to explain," I asked calmly, gazing at Freddie like I could read the answers on her face. She reacted the second I pressed her, genuine emotion rising on her face. Like Crispin, her pale skin showed her every feeling.

"What happened, Freddie? I need to understand what happened."

Freddie's voice grew more frantic and tears welled in her eyes. The night their parents died. Freddie had been there. She knew what happened to them.

The biggest secret in the British media was slowly unraveling in a tiny cottage in the English countryside. I glanced at Katrina, wondering if Freddie ought to trust her. Katrina killed someone and they knew. That inspired a type of trust, I supposed.

Freddie continued nervously, "That night... I planned on telling Crispin everything that happened to me. I had proof and everything but I didn't want him to remember. I just wanted to practice drugging someone. I just wanted to believe that I could go through with it. August wasn't supposed to be home."

She sounded crazy, but I had felt crazy at some points during my upbringing. Nothing had ever pushed me to that point, but Freddie was clearly different. While her story moved me and made me feel numb all the way down to my core, it barely had any effect on Crispin.

"You weren't supposed to be in town," Crispin said sternly.

"Daddy sent me away for my third treatment," Freddie whispered. "I worked out a way to come back for the weekend. I knew this time, he wanted me locked up for good. He knew I wanted to talk. Crispin never knew and neither did Mum. But she found out. Before I could tell Crispin, she'd gone into my room looking for pills and she'd found my journal. When Crispin and I came back from the pub… we heard her screaming."

"I don't remember any of this," Crispin whispered.

"Then don't," she snapped. "It doesn't matter anyway. They won't let me get far and when they find me, they'll punish me. I'll go to prison for what I did and for what August did too."

"To be fair, I didn't know he was a monster when I fell for him," Katrina said.

Freddie glared at her and muttered, "I wish you'd have an abortion."

"Don't wish your sinful choice on me," said Katrina. "Every baby is a gift. Even this one."

Freddie looked sickened to her stomach. Katrina could still be perfectly calloused, making it hard to remember that I did ultimately sympathize with her. She was broken too. Probably more broken than any of us realized.

"Mum was screaming at Dad. August wasn't supposed to be home, but he was there. And Mum was screaming at him too."

She set her tea down and wiped her tears as she warbled, "Daddy said something to August. He nodded and then… he took… he took the statue. He must have hit her. I'd gone running because of what I heard. Crispin could barely stand, but I tried to drag him along. August was so angry…"

She paused for a moment, then Freddie said certainly, "August killed our mother."

A tear formed in the corner of Crispin's eye.

"She didn't deserve that," he whispered. "She tried to protect us."

"She tried to protect *you*," said Freddie. "You were her

precious blond little boy. Not a nightmare like me or a twat like August."

"I don't understand how everything escalated," I asked, intervening before Crispin could say something particularly cruel. I watched his jaw clench and saw all the danger signs for Crispin saying something completely insensitive.

"I only wanted to kill dad and August but everything got out of control..."

Crispin's jaw clenched and he folded his arms.

"Crispin couldn't stand the screaming and he broke away from me," Freddie said. "He could barely walk but he just had to get in the middle. He lunged for Dad. August lunged for me. I don't know how but I got away from him. Crispin was hurt. He was on his back and Dad was punching him. I kept yelling at him to stop and he wouldn't... I killed Dad. A lot."

"You smashed his head beyond recognition," Crispin snarled.

"Then August smashed our mother's properly," Freddie whispered. "After she died. It's why I didn't want to escape until now. You're fucking lucky you don't remember that."

"You drugged me..."

"You were on the floor. August was screaming. Then you got angry with me. You didn't want to believe that August or Dad could do something like that. The drugs must have been... bad or the stress of everything. You were screaming at us and calling us monsters. You pushed me and then you..." Freddie whimpered. "You tried to kill me."

"I don't remember that."

"August stopped you. I think to save his own skin. He

forced you to drink more and then he took me into his bedroom and…"

Freddie stopped talking and we didn't need more time to know what happened.

"I don't care about what August did to me," she whispered. "I care about what he took. That's why Gran is having the bodies exhumed. I convinced them that I buried it in my letters, but the truth is, I have no idea where it could be."

"What did they take?" I asked, barely making sense of the story. Buried it in her letters? Crispin and Freddie seemed to have a twin language that was outside of my comprehension.

"A little black book," Crispin said. "Metaphorically. It's a hard drive."

"I've spent my entire life abused and sold by my own father," said Freddie. "Some of the most powerful men in Britain, America, Canada and Europe have come to the Pink Plantation parties. If Mum had just waited… I would have taken them all down. That's what I wanted."

"You should have told me earlier," Crispin snapped.

His sister hit back with a harsher critique, "You were too busy pining over girls or taking drugs to worry about your freak sister."

"What was I meant to believe? You fucked every girl I ever liked since before I knew what sex *was*. I didn't know what they were doing to you. I would have never tolerated it and I'm not going to tolerate it now."

Freddie's voice grew harsh and she reminded me so much of her brother as she snarled, "What are you going to do? I don't know where the drive is and neither do you. August took it. It had to have been him. The only people who might know where it is are demon-spawn over here or the girl you sent to prison."

"Daniella won't help us. That's exactly why I framed her," Crispin snarled. "She has access to the Friedrich archives and she won't budge. She's loyal to her family, even after all the abuse."

"How did you pull that off?" Freddie asked. I would have asked the same question if I wasn't spiraling trying to piece all the details together.

"Lawyers and money," Crispin said. "The usual way."

Nothing about this felt real. How could he have framed Daniella when she could have just confessed? That was where the money came in, I supposed. But that didn't explain everything else. What were the Friedrich archives? Why didn't anything they said make sense?

"Stop," I said. "Please. Can all of you shut up?"

Crispin froze. He hadn't looked at me in several minutes.

"I need to understand this," I said. "And I need you to tell me if I have anything wrong. Freddie. Your brother, dad and grandfather sexually abused you along with other girls. Other men were involved. Correct?"

Freddie nodded and then uncomfortably poured herself another cup of tea.

"August killed your mother and Freddie killed your father. But she only did it in self-defense! Can't you just go to the police?"

Freddie rolled her eyes, a hint of irritation that reminded me of Crispin crossing her face.

"Is she stupid?" She whispered.

"Don't insult her," Crispin snarled.

"Amina, babe," Crispin said, putting his hand on my

shoulder, "We're talking about some of the most powerful men in Britain. My grandfather isn't the only one who wants Freddie institutionalized. Her medical bills are too expensive for the estate to manage alone. I've looked into the records and they costs are insane. Drugs, security, GPS tracking. Just breaking her out of there required bringing Barnaby Fox into the mix. It's all in the money, isn't it? Because of John I've been looking into the money and... I bloody hate maths. Benjamin's better with numbers. He's helping. But very powerful people want Freddie locked up. We don't know who they are or just how powerful. But we can guess."

"If you go to the police, you'll all be killed," Katrina said. "Trust me."

"Why should anyone trust you?" I snapped at Katrina. Sorry, but I was still bitter.

"Because. I'm a Barclay bitch. I had an affair with their dad when I was fourteen," she said, almost as if she was bragging. But her face never lit up and her eyes just looked... dead.

Crispin winced and Freddie resumed her tapping more furiously.

"It wasn't an affair," Crispin whispered. "It was rape."

"Yeah. Well. That's not how my dad saw it. And his punishment was... severe."

"What punishment?"

"None of your bloody business," Katrina answered testily. She was getting on my damn nerves, but I didn't want to add more problems to my life than I already had by letting Katrina get under my skin more than necessary.

She was still a liar, which pissed me off more than her rudeness.

I snapped at her, "You weren't even a virgin before August?"

"Don't you get it?" Katrina snapped. "Unlike you, I don't want everyone running around behind my back calling me a whore and talking about my traumatic past. The best way to get away from this is to just pretend it never happened to me."

"So lie to yourself as well as everyone else?"

"I'm not a slut. I didn't choose to lose my virginity. I deserve to be Katrina the virgin. Not Katrina the knocked up skank. I'm not like you who opens her legs for everyone."

"You have some nerve saying that to me."

"I don't mean your dad," Katrina huffed. "But Devin? Come on. How easy are you?"

"At least I'm not stupid enough to have a baby when I could have easily had an abortion," I snapped.

I knew it was insensitive, but Katrina had said and done worse to me. This was better than smacking her smug ass face. She could get under my nerves like no other person.

"You still lied to all your friends. You still put me through the same shit you said you didn't want to go through," I continued. "You humiliated me, shamed me and excluded me. You treated me like a slut."

Crispin looked at me like he was surprised I had this much to say. White boy, I had been holding back with Katrina for a long time.

Katrina's cheeks puffed out angrily and her nostrils flared as she sneered, "Well not all of us can handle the entire world hating us! I grew up with parents who didn't pay me any mind. And then a man... my friend's dad started touching me and... doing other things to me. It felt good. I let him do horrific things to me because I was such a… I was weak. I'm not like you, Amina. I couldn't stay weak. I can't just be a frail wisp of a girl falling into the arms of a boy."

"I'm not a frail wisp," I hissed.

Katrina gave me a smug, disbelieving little look.

"Really? Think I don't know why you starve yourself? I get it. I just choose to be strong."

"Lying isn't strong. Being cruel isn't strong," I snapped.

"It's the only way I know how to survive," Katrina said. "As a black woman, you ought to understand."

"Don't pull that card with me when you're ashamed to be black."

"You don't even know what it means to be black," Katrina snapped. "At least I've got black parents."

"So do I! It's not my fault I don't know my biological parents. How can you come for me for being adopted?"

"Adopted or not, you ruin all the black girls' reputations by sleeping around and broadcasting your sexual past," Katrina said. "Seriously, Amina. You think Vi Bainbridge doesn't secretly think you're a slut?"

"Vi's a real friend, unlike you."

"I'm more real than Vi. I'll tell you what people really think."

Freddie raised her eyebrows and Crispin kept pensively staring at his giant feet.

"I can't be in the same room with you," I snapped at Katrina. I tried running away, but Crispin's hand cupped my waist and I found myself circling back to him.

Freddie sighed.

"Try knowing her during the awkward secondary school phase…"

Crispin's arm tightened around my shoulder. I wanted to throw him off me, but I couldn't bring myself to do it.

"The hard drive has proof of everything my father did to Freddie and everyone else he hurt," Crispin said. "Someone took it before the police got there. August drugged Freddie after I passed out and had his people hospitalize her again. Katrina searched through August's things after his funeral last year and couldn't find them. Freddie misdirected my grandparents to dig up my parents bodies…"

I didn't understand why Freddie had to do something that morbid as a misdirection, but I had a very different understanding of family than the Barclays did.

"And there is a hard drive with a list of the most powerful people in the world and details about their offshore bank accounts that they use to traffic children and teen girls around the world," Freddie finished.

"There was someone else in the house that night," Crispin whispered. "But I've done everything to remember who it was. It had to have been someone close to the family. Someone very close…"

"I remember everything perfectly. I would have remembered."

"Except you wouldn't," Crispin snapped. "You and August left and I woke up. I found them. I didn't even know what I was looking at. I might not remember what happened before they died, but I can't forget the smell in the morning or the blood on the carpets."

"That's why you think someone else was in the house?" I added.

"It's a sense," he said, shrugging. I didn't think that was a good explanation. Maybe it was a suppressed memory.

83

Freddie gave her brother a sympathetic look. Crispin's chest heaved and he stopped gripping the counter long enough to put another cigarette between his lips.

"Seriously? I'm pregnant," Katrina said. "Quit smoking."

Crispin grunted miserably and put the cigarette out in the ash tray.

"Could it be John?" I squeaked.

"Your dad?" Crispin asked, confused.

"No, dummy. John Braithwaite. Maybe he came to the house. Maybe he has it."

"Why wouldn't John have told me?" Crispin said.

Oh, Crispin. He had so many secrets, you'd think he could guess that he wasn't the only one.

"Because he thinks you killed your parents," I said. "Or something. Maybe. I don't know."

I wasn't sure if I was right... but something felt right about this. I was still furious with Crispin for lying, but I didn't know if I could truly blame him for lying either. He thought the secrets were too dark for me and he didn't want me involved in a crime that went so deep and touched on so many issues that tortured my mind. Crispin cared enough to try to protect me from reminders of my traumatic past.

But I had gone looking for trouble and my discovery chilled me to my damn core. *Why did I go looking for trouble like this?*

Freddie sat with her thin legs crossed like a translucent praying mantis and she stirred her tea and glanced between them for answers or more suggestions about what might have happened. Crispin's jaw tightened and moved nervously back and forth. I exhaled slowly, staring at Crispin, and waiting patiently for someone to say anything at all.

Chapter Ten

Freddie wrinkled her nose and waited for Crispin to respond. I folded my arms, shifting my weight from one leg to another as I searched his face for answers. If he had any better theories, he didn't share them. He just stroked his chin and shrugged.

"I'll talk to John," Crispin said. "He'll tell the truth if I'm straightforward."

Katrina made an irritated groan.

"I hate being pregnant," she said, stretching out and clutching her stomach with a constipated expression on her face. We had gone too long without talking about her, I supposed.

"You can always kill the demon spawn," Freddie muttered.

Crispin glared at his twin sister while I tried not to laugh at Freddie's dark suggestion. She was obviously joking.

"Don't. That's our brother's child..." Crispin warned her, although the wicked idea awakened a strangely gleeful expression on Freddie's face. Crispin's warning barely seemed to affect her.

"Right. Because Gran will be so happy with both of you for your romantic choices."

Crispin's cheeks darkened and he moved closer to me. I was still frozen, thinking about John and everything I'd heard from them.

"John could be another victim," Freddie admitted. I guessed that she meant a victim of August or her father, but I didn't think so. When you went through trauma the way I did, you could almost tell who else had gone through what you did. I could almost read Freddie's thoughts about her trauma and I could definitely understand the fucked up way she saw the world.

I didn't sense that type of darkness in John Brathwaite.

Katrina perked up a bit at the mention of a new man's name.

"Is John hot?" Katrina asked, fluffing out her hair like he was around the corner. I struggled not to roll my eyes. Didn't she have more important things to worry about than impressing a guy right now?

"He's black," Freddie said neutrally.

"Oh, I don't mind black guys," Katrina said, as if this were a startling revelation.

"Katrina, *you're* black," I said.

She shrugged and thankfully, Crispin interrupted before I could tear into her again.

"I'll work on this. I'll leave the two of you alone. I need to discuss this with my girlfriend."

"Your girlfriend?" Freddie said. "Seriously? Melodramatic, much?"

"Shut up," Crispin snarled.

His grasp tightened around my wrist and he pulled me to the cottage's master bedroom. The sheets were messy and his clothes were all over the bed. There was a football on the desk and pages of paper ripped up and crumpled around it. Once we were alone, Crispin slumped against the wall, hunching the way tall boys did when they were tired of sticking up like reeds and didn't want to be seen anymore.

"I'm sorry."

"You covered up a murder," I said, attempting to release the weight of it but finding the heaviness continuing to wrap itself around my heart. Crispin could barely look me in the eye which only made the situation worse. I yearned for his eye contact. And more.

"Yes… I covered up a murder," he said simply. My chest tightened. Why did I want his arms around me after what I just learned?

"And you know who killed your parents," I replied. My voice felt like it was softer than normal, and more gentle. Like I was submitting to the idea that I was head over heels in love with someone who could embrace something so dark. I wanted to run headfirst into his darkness, contrary to my previous opinion.

"Yes…" Crispin replied.

"Why are you letting the press trash your name? Why are you taking the fall for this?"

"Because it's Freddie. It's my duty to protect her. It's my duty to protect anyone weaker than me."

"Is that why you keep chasing me? Because you think I'm weaker."

"You are weaker," he said fiercely. I hated him for saying

it, even if it was true. It didn't feel fair that he should point it out. I didn't choose to be this small.

"Screw you, Crispin."

"Physically, at least," he said softly and unapologetically. "I can't deny that, Twiggy. You're tiny. Breakable. I ought to protect you too."

"I can't process all this right now."

"Right."

"I came through your window to talk about our relationship," I said, suddenly feeling like our silly college relationship was insignificant compared to traumatic pasts and little black books. Crispin's ears perked up when I mentioned our relationship.

"What do you want?"

"I thought I knew what I wanted when I climbed in the window," I replied. "Now, I don't know what the hell is happening."

"I told you the truth, Amina. If it's too much for you, I will respectfully let you go... and murder anyone who touches you until we graduate."

"You wouldn't kill Devin," I said.

"You'd go back to Devin!?"

"No! My point is. He's touched me. He's alive."

"For now..." Crispin said ominously, raising a single dark eyebrow to at least have plausible deniability that he'd been joking.

"What are you going to do now?"

"The John theory... and... hopefully..."

He met my gaze but he didn't finish his sentence. I couldn't take my eyes off him. My big bad Barclay.

"Hopefully what?" I whispered.

"Make love to you."

"We can't do that now."

"Why not?"

I touched his cheek. Why not? Good question, Crispin. Why not? We just spent the night talking about your deep dark secrets which include secrets about high profile murders and a ring of child predators.

All that ran through my head, but what I could muster was, "Um…"

His fingers rushed to my hips and he clenched tightly and instinctively. I was getting exactly what I wanted. The closeness I yearned for made my heart race. I leaned into it and more importantly, I leaned into Crispin's strong, physical form. *He's so goddamn beautiful.*

"I love you. Nothing about that is different," he whispered.

At least I had certainty about one thing. Crispin's love. And because of his confession, his innocence.

"You're not a killer," I said with relief.

"Probably not."

Why were my fingers still on Crispin's jawline? And why did gazing into his eyes make me feel like this? His fingers clutched me tighter.

"Probably?" I muttered. Crispin didn't reply.

"I want you back," he said. "I'll do anything."

"No killing people."

He tilted his head back, blond hair cascading away from his face.

"Right," he whispered.

His accent was perfect. So was his neck. My hips moved closer to him and I pressed against him, holding onto him properly now.

"We shouldn't do this."

"Yeah, babe. Totally."

He kissed me. I knew he would kiss me. Crispin hadn't exactly been subtle. He held onto my hips and pulled me against him forcefully as he kissed me. I grabbed onto him, squeezing Crispin's enormous biceps and then roughly pulling him away from the wall.

Crispin made a low growling sound in his throat before he grabbed my hips and lifted me against the wall. He had to bend so his head wouldn't brush the low ceiling at the bedroom's entrance. He carried me over to the bed and gently lay me back, his lips teasing my shoulders and then trailing down my chest as he ripped my clothes off.

I'd been unsuccessfully struggling to peel Crispin's clothes off. Once he had me naked, he gazed at me lovingly, the bulge between his legs grew even more rigid. His tongue unconsciously darted over his lower lip as he removed his belt and stripped his shirt off. Crispin's body looked incredible. I'd missed it. He crawled between my legs, kissing me as his hair fell over his face.

"I love you, Twiggy."

My heart flipped again. I wanted his love even if it scared me. My love for Crispin didn't feel healthy. It was a non-stop addictive rush when we were together. But when we were apart, I felt worse. I yearned for moments like these. I pressed my body against Crispin's allowing myself to feel his warmth and love.

"I know," I whispered, grabbing his jawline and feeling an unusual prickling of stubble across his face. I liked the stubble and raked my fingers over it as Crispin moved his hips so he could press his bulge against me. His eyes fixed on me, making me feel so damn special.

"I want you," he said. I could feel myself forgetting all my hesitation and going back to him, even if I knew he was still completely deranged and tortured from his past. So was I.

I tangled my fingers in my hair as I kissed him. Yes. I wanted him too.

"Okay," I whispered. "I want you too."

"Good," he whispered. "Do you want me to kiss you?"

"Yes…"

"What else?" Crispin whispered, kissing my nose and then running his thumb slowly over my lower lips. He shuddered as he touched my lips and I moved my body even closer to his than before.

"More…"

"Like what?" he asked with a glimmer of mischief coloring his perfectly chiseled face.

"I want to fuck…" I whimpered. I didn't know why my voice came out so damn weak, but it entertained the hell out of Crispin. He chuckled.

"Oh, sweetheart. I'm absolutely *not* having sex with you unless you're my girlfriend again."

"What?"

I pushed against his chest but Crispin was rigid and immovable against my tiny fists. I scowled at him.

"This is so unfair…"

"No. It's not unfair. I have feelings too… And I want my girl back."

"What if I don't want you back?" I said, even if I knew it was stupid. I obviously wanted Crispin back. I missed him. I missed our conversations, our kisses and the way he cared about me. Guys didn't care about girls that way. I wanted those moments on the beach in Barbados. I needed to wake up on his chest. I imagined an entire future with Crispin and I couldn't picture waking up every day without him next to me. But… *he still scared me.*

"Then dump me again."

My heart fluttered and I shook my head. I didn't want to do that. He lured me back in again. Maybe I'd done it to myself. I didn't know which magnet you were supposed to blame when two magnets fastened themselves together.

"No," I breathed weakly.

Crispin moved his body against mine, raising my arousal slowly. "So you're taking me back?"

"Yes…"

"Ugh…" he groaned, pressing his lips to my forehead. "You are so difficult."

"Shut up, white boy."

"Okay, black girl…"

"That sounds wrong," I whispered, pulling his face to mine.

Processing. This was processing. Kissing. Touching. Doing everything except having sex. Crispin didn't need sex to make me cum. When we were finally thoroughly satisfied, Crispin pulled my sweaty body against his and he twirled his fingers around my hair.

"Don't scare me again," I whispered. "Please…"

"I won't," Crispin said. "I won't. I swear…"

There was enough kissing for me to forget the pain. He was always an incredible kisser and the yearning Crispin felt for me only made it better. I let him do whatever the hell he wanted to me. I wanted his lips all over my body. Crispin pulled away to keep talking. My breath couldn't slow down.

"So... I know we just got back to school but... what do you think about the Easter holiday in Barbados?"

"As long as my dad doesn't get there."

"He'll be running for president," Crispin sighed.

"And my mom's in England. Somewhere."

"Really?" Crispin said, sitting up suddenly. Why the heck was he so interested in my mom?

"Yeah. Who cares? She says she's leaving my dad but I don't even believe her."

Crispin chewed on his lower lip for a few moments.

"Your mum messaged me."

"Huh?"

"Email. I dunno how she got it, but she did."

I could feel another heavy cloud hovering over me. Frances could be out of line, but messaging my boyfriend?

The Hewetts were always closing in on me – threatening my independence. At the risk of shattering the softness that just built up between us, I asked Crispin, "What did the email say?"

Chapter Eleven

My mom went behind my back to try to get Crispin to convince me to talk to her. I couldn't tell if she was drunk in her email to him or just being a typical awkward mom.

She wanted to see me and Crispin thought she'd been confused. Now that we were talking about her, his gaze fixed on mine and it was like his problems disappeared and mine were the only ones that mattered. He told me that she emailed him days before school started, which explained why he hadn't mentioned it right away. Ugh.

Just knowing she would reach out to him made me feel violated. Crispin kept his concerned gaze fixated on me directly.

"Do you *want* to see her?" he asked. Obviously, the answer to that was no.

"Don't we have more important things to talk about."

"Nothing and no one is more important to me than you."

With his body pressed against mine, believing Crispin was dangerously easy. Why wouldn't I want to believe that I was the most important thing to my extremely hot blond boyfriend?

"Tell me you won't kill anyone."

"I can't promise that. I still want to kill your dad."

"Pack it up, Lee Harvey Oswald."

"He's not going to win," Crispin said certainly, but we both knew that he couldn't be certain and that from this point on, killing my dad was completely out of the question. This would be a terrible time to attract attention to myself since my dad's run for president would mean the media crawling all over him. I ran my hands over Crispin's chest. Instead of thinking about gross creeps like my dad, I wanted to think about Crispin's firm chest and his invitation to go back to Barbados with him.

The thought of facing his grandparents again worried me.

"I don't want them to know I'm back, so we won't stay at the plantation," he whispered as if he could read my mind.

"Your apartment?"

"Yes. But you may have to be willing to travel rough for a bit."

"What does *that* mean?"

"No fancy cars, no private planes. I'm going incognito."

"I fly on regular planes all the time," I said. "Daddy prefers First Class though."

Crispin chuckled and touched my cheek.

"First class. I like a woman with standards."

I tiptoed up to him and kissed his lips. Yeah, I wanted Crispin back. Really badly. Kissing him reminded me of how much I liked him. He'd lied. Yes, he'd lied so much. But I could forgive so many other people. Why shouldn't I forgive Crispin?

I admitted, "I wanted you back for a long time."

"Finally you admit it," he said, kissing me deeply. I must have been as dumb as a chinchilla on ketamine to dump this man. He was *such* a good kisser.

"I want to feel you…" I whispered.

"Absolutely not," he said in his gruff, posh voice. "I'm taking my time with you tonight, Twiggy. I had to delay my gratification. I see no reason why you shouldn't delay yours…"

I needed him so desperately.

"We can't have hours of sex with Katrina and your twin sister on the other side of our door…"

"Why not? I want you. I need you…"

He pressed his finger to my lower lips and grinned at me.

"I *knew* you'd take me back."

I hit his chest and Crispin laughed.

"I love you, babe. And you love me. I scared you. I get it. But you've taught me a lesson," he said.

"Have I?"

He kissed me and then murmured, "Sure. Want to beat me up again?"

"I always want to beat you up…"

Crispin chuckled and then his grasp on my waist tightened.

"Too bad. Tonight, I'm torturing you…"

I couldn't fight him off this time. Not like I was trying. I was mostly giggling and offering up fake resistance as he tied my hands behind my back with his belt and then propped my legs open. He didn't take my clothes off or anything yet. My lower back balanced on my clasped hands as Crispin got off the bed and stared at me all tied up. I rolled over and looked at him staring at me. He bit his lower lip and breathed, "You're beautiful."

"Thanks."

He nodded and smiled again before sliding between my legs and touching the waist of my jeans.

"I'll have these off now."

I edged my hips up toward him and he ran his fingers over my waist.

"What Freddie says isn't exactly true. I don't like thin girls in general. I like you. There's something to appreciate in every woman."

He pushed my shirt up a little and kissed the top of my stomach. He shuddered after kissing me.

"You're warm, Lips."

"So are you."

"No. Not like you…"

He pulled my jeans down a little more and touched my hips.

"I like your hips. I like your tummy. I like everything. I missed all of it."

He tugged at the top of my underwear with his teeth. A sharp exhalation of his warm breath made me squirm with anticipation. Crispin was slowing everything down to his undeniably patient pace. I bucked my hips up again, willing him to rip my underwear off with his teeth or do something crazy and sexy like that. Not like being tied up wasn't crazy and sexy. Crispin rolled my jeans off and now he had the tops of my thighs and my legs at his disposal. He finally kissed the top of my mound through my underwear.

He kissed my thighs and then kissed his way back up to

his lips. He hovered over me and couldn't help but pressing his hips against me.

"I like having you tied up and calm… and mine…"

He bent his lips to my neck and sucked on my flesh. *Hard.* I moaned and pressed my body against his. He chuckled and grabbed my hips.

"Fuck yeah, babe. Now that's a moan."

He sucked on my neck again and I whimpered, squirming against him. His ticklish kisses and the gentle sucking on my neck were both driving me wild. Crispin put his hand against my underwear and groaned.

"You are so fucking wet…"

"I'm not… you don't even turn me on…" I teased.

Crispin tugged at my lower lip between his teeth and whispered, "Liar…"

I giggled as he kissed my neck fiercely again. He rubbed me slowly outside my underwear, teasing me with what was to come. When Crispin finally slipped his hand inside my underwear, I was soaked. His large fingers spread me apart as he covered them in my juices and then moved them to his lips.

"You taste good, babe."

He kissed his way down my stomach again and then he ripped my underwear off with his teeth. He did it so fast that I didn't realize what was happening until I felt the scraping tug of fabric against my skin and then the erotic softness of Crispin's tongue spreading my lower lips open immediately afterward.

He didn't miss a beat. His tongue was inside me and *deep* before I could react. I couldn't react, really. He'd tied my hands up. I moaned and moved my hips toward him. Crispin grabbed my hips and licked furiously between my legs like he was trying to lick me clean. I couldn't stop myself from getting close to an orgasm faster than ever.

I'd wanted him so badly, I was so wet and Crispin was *extremely* talented at finding sensitive spots between my legs and teasing them in just the right way. When I finally climaxed, he cupped my ass cheeks and pressed me into his face, continuing to suck on my clit until I came again... and again... I forgot about the danger of being heard and just cared about my pleasure. I tried to be quiet, but I didn't know or care if it was enough. I lost myself in the pleasure of being with Crispin.

By the time he finished eating me out, I didn't think I could handle his dick. I suddenly remembered that he was insanely big and I was tiny. We always had to go slow but then I remembered how good he felt and how amazing and totally pleasurable it was to feel Crispin's big cock like a knot in the base of my stomach while he made me cum repeatedly.

I wanted to push his head away from my crotch and drag him over to me. With bound hands, I settled for eye contact. Crispin sat across from me and grinned.

"You look ready for it."

"Yes," I whispered. "I am. We're back together. We're all good. Let's have sex."

"No."

"What?"

"I said I was delaying your gratification. Bit of a doormat if you ask me, since I ate you out."

"That wasn't sex, though."

"Hm... yes it was. You came. That's sex."

"What about you?"

"I've waited this long," he said smugly. "What's a little longer?"

"Is this your twisted idea of punishing me?"

"Yes."

"I'll break you, white boy," I teased.

He leaned over and kissed my forehead.

"I'm sure you will, Lips," he whispered. "Promise you won't kill me when I untie you?"

"Take your chances," I whispered back.

"Fair enough."

Chapter Twelve

In the morning, I smelled bacon and knew Crispin was making breakfast. I didn't dread the idea of breakfast for a change. I got out of bed and hurried out there. Freddie was already sitting at the table. She looked a bit like Crispin when he barely slept, with dark circles under her eyes. When Freddie saw me, she smirked.

"Someone had a good night."

"Shut up," Crispin said.

"Sound travels. Unfortunately. I'd rather *not* think about Crispin… you know… shagging…"

She made a gagging sound and I secretly wished the ground would open me up and swallow me whole. I bent my head and grumbled an awkward greeting. Crispin pinched Freddie on the shoulder and she yelped.

"Leave her alone."

"Pinch me again and I'll stomp your bollocks you psychopath," she hissed.

"Yeah? Takes one to know one, doesn't it."

"More coffee, darling?" Freddie asked me in a purposefully affected manner. I hadn't had any coffee to begin with, so I nodded. Freddie poured me a cup and Crispin folded bacon off the cast-iron pan onto our plates. He served us up bacon, eggs, toast and baked beans before sitting with a huff.

"No sausages?"

"Stop making bloody demands and eat."

"I haven't had this much to eat in ages. Mental hospital food. It sucks."

I nodded sympathetically. My mouth-watered just staring at the plate. Crispin really must have been having an effect on me, because I went straight for the beans and toast. If my stupid dad was going to become President of the United States, I'd probably have to get used to being British. I'd be like the reverse Meghan Markle on the run...

Crispin ate his entire slice of toast in one bite, stretching his mouth open like a snake while Freddie gawked in horror.

"Christ. I feel so sorry for the heterosexuals. I don't know how you could be attracted to them. They're such beasts."

"Shut up, Freddie," Crispin said in a garbled voice through his mouthful of bread.

"Where's Katrina?" I asked after a few more sips of coffee. Freddie rolled her eyes and Crispin managed to choke out that she was still sleeping. I didn't know if I wanted to see Katrina this morning.

"Freddie will lay low here for a while. I'll take you two back to school."

"What about Daniella?"

"What about her?" Crispin said.

"She didn't kill August."

"I know. There's not much I can do about that now, can I?"

"Tell the truth. Sink Katrina."

"Oh, I like her," Freddie muttered.

"Katrina's part of our family now. It doesn't matter what you all think. It's still important to be a Barclay. And a Hargreaves."

"Why?" Freddie asked.

I hated to agree with Crispin's twin sister. Did Crispin seriously expect Katrina to be a good mom? She didn't care about other people. She *killed* her baby's father. Even if she had good reasons, it was still a little toxic to murder someone.

Crispin's back stiffened and he rolled his shoulders to try to relax himself.

"Firstly," he said, mimicking a calm he certainly didn't feel, "Our heritage and our family are important whether we like it or not. We're in the news. We're descended from some of Britain's wealthiest planters and merchants. What we do with that legacy matters. I'm not saying we should be posh wankers. We *are* posh wankers without even trying. But maybe we could do something better."

Freddie looked at her brother like he had two heads. The words stumbled out of my mouth before I had a chance to speak, "Didn't you try to kill someone like... two weeks ago?"

Crispin shrugged.

"I'm not perfect."

"He really isn't," Freddie said.

"Quiet," Crispin muttered bitterly. "I'm letting you stow away here *and* you're using my accounts so you can avoid detection. Considering the number of Chanel boxes you've stashed under the sink, I'd be grateful."

103

"How long have you been here?" I asked her.

Freddie rolled her eyes.

"A week. He acts like it's not boring. I asked him to bring a girl for me. Or a guy."

"I thought you didn't—

"Well, girls are better. But boys are okay in a pinch."

"I guess it really is a spectrum," I said awkwardly.

Crispin glanced at Freddie and then at me.

"We'd better go. I'll wake Katrina."

"Are you going to leave me here all day?"

"I'll send you a stripper gram," Crispin grumbled.

He stormed off and I polished off the last sips of my coffee and food. Freddie was quiet. She had a far off look in her eye and I didn't want to interrupt her thinking. She was like a different person, almost. Not bubbly or snarky anymore. She smiled at me as if she were smiling through me until Crispin came back with an extremely grouchy Katrina in tow. She still had her bonnet on and sweatpants. She glowered at Crispin.

"Why are you up so bloody early?"

"Don't you have classes?"

"I'm pregnant. All I care about is prayer, Bible study, my baby, and fantasizing about when I can drink vodka again."

Crispin pursed his lips nervously. I gave him a look that said "I told you so" but he only grunted awkwardly and ushered us both out the door. I sat in the front with Crispin and Katrina sat in the back, pulling a wool blanket over her head and groaning pathetically. Crispin glanced back at her and then gave me an apologetic look. Yeah. He had a lot to be sorry for, but I wanted to forgive him. I reached over and pushed some of his blond hair out of his face, kissing his cheek before he drove.

Katrina slept the whole way. We dropped her off a few feet from L.R. Crispin insisted on coming into L.C. With me.

"Mandeep's cool, you said?" He asked, stuffing his hands into his pockets and zipping up his hoodie before throwing the hood over his head.

"Yeah. She's a better roommate than Katrina. She came clean to me about coming onto you and everything."

"Right."

We stopped outside the door and I crossed my arms.

"You don't have to come in with me. It's not even allowed."

"Mandeep wouldn't mind, you said. And I think we ought to talk some more. Last night was heavy. I wouldn't blame you if you changed your mind."

"I'm not dumping you again. Not after last night."

Crispin chuckled and wriggled his brows suggestively.

"Was I that good with my tongue?"

"Shut up."

Crispin grabbed my waist and pulled me close to him. Kissing him felt phenomenal again. I pressed my hands against his chest and allowed myself to lean into his weight. We were kissing really hard when the front door of LC flung open. I yelped and we pulled away. Mandy stood in the doorway, dressed in her pajamas, and totally bewildered.

"Amina. Crispin. Stay out here. Shhh."

She pressed her fingers to her lips and covered our mouths. I gave her a confused look.

"Amina, I didn't want to bring it up because I myself have been the subject of nasty rumors but... I heard through the grapevine what happened last semester and... I..."

"Spit it out!" I whispered.

"Your mum's in our room. I've been distracting her and pretending that you're playing tennis with Vi. Paige has been on watch duty over there so I can get to you before you come back. I'm guessing you two have a complicated relationship."

"How much do people on this campus gossip?" I grumbled. What the hell did my mom want? It was bad enough that she emailed Crispin but showing up here was pushing all my boundaries and worrying me. I didn't want her to make a habit out of trying to get close to me.

Mandy gave me a sympathetic smile. Wow. The girls in LC already knew all my secrets and they'd still been sweet to me. Maybe it wasn't such a bad thing to know that they'd heard Ella's version of the truth and chosen to believe mine. I regretted not giving Katrina a good kick in the leg back at the cottage for *her* comments. Crispin probably would have stopped me, but it would have been worth a try. And he probably only would have stopped me because she was pregnant.

"To be fair, tell Trevor anything and he'll make it sound ten times worse when he tells the next person," Mandy continued.

Crispin scowled and snarled, "I'll handle things, Mandy. Thank you."

Mandy gazed up at him like he was a celebrity and not just a really tall (but sexy) freak of nature. I glanced up at Crispin, seeing if he would ask me what I wanted. Naturally, he didn't.

"Happy to help," she said cheerily to Mandeep.

I didn't know what I wanted, anyway. Crispin took my hand and led me into my dorm.

"Crispin, should we slow down?"

"Why?" he said. "Every time she comes near you, she throws off your progress by making you freeze up. I'm handling this."

"I just…"

"No," he snarled. "How dare your mother come here? I'm ending this."

He stormed off toward my dorm room, dragging me along.

Chapter Thirteen

Frances' knobby knees locked together, her legs sealed shut and her upper back stiff as she considered my room with a judgmental gaze.

"Where's all the pink stuff I got you?" She said as I walked into the room with Crispin behind me. Her lips pursed.

"We pay good money to make sure boys aren't allowed to come in here and molest you whenever they please."

I wanted to scream, "Hoe, why is you here?!"

Instead, I leaned against Crispin and folded my arms.

"I don't want to see you. I told you I didn't want to see you."

"I'm your mother. As long as I'm your legal guardian—"

"I'm eighteen. You're nobody's legal guardian. Now move."

Frances' blue eyes flickered with frustration. She knew better than to go out of her way to upset me.

"I'm not leaving until you talk to me. You're my daughter. I made mistakes, Amina. I know I have… and I'm sorry."

"You called me a slut five seconds after I told you that Daddy raped me. I'm done with your cracker ass!"

Frances flinched. I never really used the insult cracker, but I knew it would bother her. Crispin raised a bemused eyebrow. My mother was anything but amused.

"I came here to offer you help and to warn you about that boy. Despite what your father says, I'm not actually stupid. I was top ten in my class at Dana Hall."

"I don't need you to warn me about Crispin. Considering you lived with a *pedophile* for the past twenty years, I don't exactly think you're a good judge of character."

My mother's lips pursed in an angry line and then she sighed, closing her eyes and attempting to find her balance.

"I am sorry. I am sorry for how he hurt you and I'm sorry for letting it happen. I came here to tell you the truth."

"The truth? You've never told me the damn truth. I know my parents are alive, Frances. I wasn't lost in the storm. Daddy *bought* me."

I shrieked it at her. Then her face lost all its color. Her black pupils nearly covered her entire iris. Her lower lip trembled. All the color rushed back to her face but this was ten times scarier than when it happened to Crispin. My mom went through more shades than I knew possible and her voice came out in a shaky whisper.

"He did what?"

"Don't act like you didn't know," Crispin snarled.

Frances continued to change color and her voice was even more of a stammering mess than usual.

"Didn't know... Amina... No. That's not possible. Your father... your father brought you to our lawyer. I was there. He said he found you. He *found* you."

She kept repeating it, like she was trying to convince herself. Crispin was glaring at her, ready to accuse her of being a liar. I knew Frances Hewett. I knew what she was like when she was lying. If she wanted to avoid a John Hewett whoop down, every once in a while she'd have to lie about how many bottles of wine she drank or how long she planned on staying in Boston with her parents, or how much she'd charged at the country club. This time, she wasn't lying.

"We have reason to believe otherwise."

Her cheeks darkened and I heard my mother say words I'd *never* heard her say before.

"Fucking bastard."

I stepped back sharply. Just as she said the words, she seemed to realize that they were most unladylike and she cleared her throat, settling back into her tight cross-legged position. She glared at Crispin.

"I knew I recognized your name and not just from the news. Your father… he was in Las Vegas… five years ago, perhaps?"

Crispin glanced at me curiously.

"Yes," he answered hesitantly.

Frances gave a self-satisfied nod, like she finally had the answer to a question that she'd asked. She turned to me and then said, "Be careful with him, Amina. Men like your father… they don't just happen in America."

Crispin put his arm around me, pulling me close.

"Amina can look after herself," he said. "She's done a good job of it so far."

Frances looked him up and down and then nodded.

"I suppose she has," she said to him.

I wanted to go to her, but I couldn't bring myself to forgive her yet. I still wanted to get her out of my bedroom.

"Why are you here, Mom?"

"That doesn't matter anymore. Your father lied to me."

"Yeah. About a lot of things."

"But not that... he... he promised me he wasn't seeing her anymore," Mom said, blubbering senselessly. I didn't know if she was talking about Ella, another mistress or a third person I hadn't thought of before.

"Seeing who? Mom can you either start making sense or start walking the hell out of here?"

She gave me a sad, sympathetic look.

"I'm sorry, honey. I need to talk to my lawyer. If you find your parents... give them my number."

"If I find them? Aren't you supposed to help me with that?"

"I'm not going to help you," she said. "I have my own problems. And you don't want me anyway..."

Her blubbering was starting to get on my nerves.

"I'm not going to give them your number. What the hell? are you out of your mind?"

Frances' eyes welled with tears.

"I have been. For a long time. For a *very* long time."

She got up and smoothed her skirts, pretending like she wasn't crying.

"Mini-me..."

"Don't call me that."

That made her tears fall. I wanted to feel sorry for her, but I couldn't. Looking at her sobbing face just made me feel numb all over again. I wasn't in control of my response to her the way I wanted to be.

"Amina…" she whispered. "My beautiful girl. I've ruined your life."

"Glad you finally understand that."

"I… If my lawyer can find out what you're saying is true, your father's presidential run is *over*."

"Great. I don't care."

"Honey. I'll be in England for a while. One of my girl-friends from Harvard is here and she's helping me work through the divorce. If you need me, I'm just a phone call away. If anyone from the press calls the school, they know what to do. I can look after you."

"Don't you get it, Frances? I don't need you. I don't want you here. I'm sorry that you and Dad are getting divorced but I can't handle your bullshit. Now *go*."

Crispin's hand grasped my shoulder firmly. Support. That's what it felt like. I didn't even feel nervous sending her packing. Frances wiped her tears and mumbled another apology before she walked off. By then, Crispin could hardly hold back. Mandy came hurrying into the room, but Crispin didn't even care that he was letting a stranger see his crazy.

"She has no right to come here," he snarled. "She's lucky I didn't —

"Crispin! She's still my mom."

"Sorry…" he muttered.

Mandy gazed up at him with stars in her eyes.

"Amina," She gasped dramatically. "He's so romantic…"

Crispin gave her a look and she looked away.

"Sorry," she muttered, like she was apologizing for making eye contact with a God. Crispin appeared completely oblivious about why she was reacting like this.

"Thanks, Mandy," he said. "We appreciate the heads up."

"Amina, are you alright?"

"I'm fine," I said, but I wasn't sure I was. Pretty sure I just broke up with my adoptive mother. It didn't feel good. She was still my only mom. She was still the person I thought would hold my hands if I ever found my birth parents. I used to dream about finding them sometimes. My mom wasn't a "welfare queen" like Dad said and my dad wasn't "homeless or in jail" either.

"Do you think she was telling the truth?" Crispin asked me. "Do you think she didn't know?"

"I know Frances. She was surprised."

"So he lied about your parents and somehow... possibly... knew my father."

"I don't know if she was telling the truth about that part."

"Coming to think of it, my father and John Hewett would have gotten along," Crispin muttered bitterly.

Mandy gave me a concerned look and wrapped her arms around me. It felt nice.

"You looked like you needed a hug," She said.

"Thanks. I totally did."

She squeezed tightly.

"If you don't mind, this evening we want to have a meeting about the sexual assault awareness campaign. Are you two free?"

"Certainly," Crispin said. "What could be more important?"

Mandy looked like she was about to gush again. I gave Crispin a stern look to calm down on the sexiness before the girl imploded. He shrugged and flashed me a winning Crispin smile. Then he leaned over and kissed my forehead.

"I'd better go make sure she isn't lurking in the bushes. Meeting later. I'll be there."

"What about… the others?"

"They're at the cottage. They're fine. I'll see you later."

He kissed me again and waltzed off. Mandy looked like she was going to burst.

"He is *incredible*. Did he tell her off?"

"A bit."

"Did you tell her off?"

"A lot."

Now, she was gushing, but she didn't press me for details. She was just… nice. Maybe that's what a real friend was. Before I could message one of my other real friends Sarah and Vi — who had been *way* better this semester — she pushed the door open.

"Jack is a bloody idiot!" Violet huffed as she stormed through the door.

"What's wrong?" I asked.

Mandy and I gathered around Vi Bainbridge who looked like she'd been crying.

"He doesn't want to help with the sexual assault awareness campaign because he thinks it'll make it look like he's guilty of sexual assault."

"What?" Mandy asked.

Girl, welcome to Jack Dyson. We are always confused.

"He's not *extremely* intelligent but no matter how I explain it to him, he just gets dumber and dumber!"

"I can get Crispin to talk to him."

"No!" Vi said. "We broke up. I'm done with that bloody idiot and his stupid football games and his stupid hair and his stupid abs and his stupid… dick…"

She broke down into sobs and I suspected that Vi wasn't "done" with Jack Dyson at all. Not yet at least.

Chapter Fourteen

Two weeks of preparing for our sexual assault awareness campaign had been a nightmare to juggle with school, Crispin and everything else going on. I still worried that any other day, I'd open my door and *boom*, Frances would be on my bed.

It was taking all of my will power not to reach out to her. I tried to tell myself that she didn't deserve to have me reach out to her out of habit. She had raised me to be completely obsessed with her – to follow in her footsteps and admire her constantly. It was like Frances wanted me to be her mom and not the other way around.

Even if I knew better, my habitual attachment to Frances was hard to break. I turned our last conversation around in my head repeatedly. Maybe she was telling the truth. I had been so sure before, but now that I had some distance from the entire situation, I could consider an alternate theory – Frances really hadn't known that Daddy bought me.

Could I possibly believe that?

Daddy had lied about a lot, but that didn't mean my adoptive mother was innocent. She was definitely fucked up in her own way, but I didn't know what to believe. Uncertainty gripped me in an unrelenting vice. I hated my inability to let my problems go. I just wanted an escape.

Crispin checked on Freddie nightly, but Katrina was back on campus and pregnancy was making her mean as hell. She was still pretending that she wasn't pregnant, of course, but she spent most of her time in the dining hall gossiping loudly. Katrina did a shockingly good job at hiding her pregnancy with very large clothes and maternity leggings. Nobody could tell her secret and she seemed more focused on social climbing and eating than anything else. Ella was her new BFF, which Vi took great offense to.

I had enough going on without paying attention to Ella, but Vi filled our text message thread with her complaints and updates about Ella. She always wore her hair down now and she wore high heels to school. Her meanness had grown worse than before and since it wasn't field hockey season, she had plenty of free time to gossip with Katrina and throw dirty looks in nearly everyone's direction.

She avoided me like I avoided her, but Ella tried to get close to Vi after sinking her claws into Katrina. If she had any evil plans, I didn't know what they were and I didn't give a crap as long as she stayed away from me.

Ella had offered to help Vi on the anti sexual assault campaign and Vi gleefully announced in our text message thread how badly she told Ella off. Her insults were a little too Shakespearean to pack a punch, but I was happy Vi got her opinions off her chest.

Unfortunately, messing with Ella had other consequences which at least told me that she hadn't learned a damn thing since the incident with Crispin – except to avoid me. Ella's goofy ass made a false report to Doukas accusing Vi of cheating on a math test which led to a public argument in the dining hall filmed by multiple people and livestreamed onto Felix Stubbins social media account.

Just before the altercation could escalate, Jack stepped between Vi and Ella, officially getting them back together. Naturally, I missed the entire event because I was anxiously avoiding the dining hall in my bedroom, temporarily slipping into my old bad habits around food.

It was nice to see Jack and Vi back together, even if working on the sexual assault awareness campaign generally made me feel like crap because of all the memories and weird feelings it brought up.

People were actually starting to *care* about the campaign. Sarah Clifford had become more militant about spreading the word, handing out pamphlets and spamming group chats and social media with information. Sarah was on a forgiveness-seeking campaign that would have impressed the pope. She even sent me a handwritten card and chocolates apologizing for all the times she'd called me a slut.

Crispin ate most of the chocolate. He'd been working out like crazy because Freddie "stressed him out". I thought he was nervous about the campaign. We were doing skits and poems and Crispin had written an essay about athletes and sexual assault to read out to the school. Crispin *hated* attention. The night before the campaign, Crispin climbed in through my window after our dorm check-ins. Mandy took her blankets and hurried off to sleep on the floor of one of the other girls' rooms. Crispin leaned against the door and beckoned me to him.

"Come here, Twiggy…"

I was still Twiggy according to Crispin, but according to my therapist and my doctor, I was finally a healthy weight. I still had to watch out for my triggers and manage my symptoms, but slowly… I was getting better. I pressed my body against Crispin's. His hair had been getting so long as we got deep into February. Sometimes he would go a day or two without shaving and get stubble on his chin as dark as his eyebrows.

Today, he'd shaved before coming over, but his long blond hair was twisted in a messy knot behind his head. I reached my fingers back, trying to get through the tangles. He chuckled and murmured, "I need a haircut."

"No… I love it."

"I feel like Tarzan."

"Sexy Tarzan…"

"Actually," Crispin said seriously. "That book was incredibly racist. I don't want you to think I condone racist literature."

"Don't worry, white boy," I whispered.

My phone buzzed on my bed, a few feet away.

"Boyfriend calling?" Crispin teased.

"Ha ha."

I glanced over.

"It's an email notification from Frances," I grumbled.

This white lady was killing my vibe. I was still on the fence about talking to her. I hadn't made up my mind and her direct contact was almost forcing the issue. I didn't want to deal with her after our fight. I didn't want conflict and I didn't want to get involved.

She could sue Daddy for all he was worth, I didn't care. It

wasn't like they could stop paying my tuition. Daddy would never make a scene like that and I didn't think he'd dare after what happened on campus last semester.

"Read it," Crispin urged.

"Um... you're here to put your dick in me, not worry about what my crusty ass mom has to say."

I reached my little hands down Crispin's pants, wrapping tightly around his big dick. He chuckled and removed my hand.

"Right," he whispered. "Except... who says I'm here to make love to you and not simply to read you poetry. And... I demand that you read her email. Now."

"Stop killing my vibe, Crispin. Mandy's sleeping on another floor tonight so I can get laid."

"Do I really get you that horny?"

"Yes..."

I scrambled for his pants again, but Crispin stopped me with his hand.

"Read it," he said sternly.

"That's why everyone says British men are boring."

"Who says that?"

"I say that."

"Girl, bye," he said, in a mocking American accent that made me gag dramatically. Crispin making fun of my accent was purely traumatizing. He always added this unnecessary twang he thought sounded Texan.

I checked the email.

To: aminahewett@rapettiacademy.co.uk

From: (Mom) francesyorkssecretemail@gmail.com

. . .

AMINA,

I AM TAKING your advice and staying far away. I've contacted my lawyers and your father knows. He will be busy on the campaign trail but you are still in trouble. **Be careful.**

I am in the company of a nice gentleman who is providing for my safety and assisting me with the divorce. Don't try to find me.

If you need me, use this address. If Daddy cuts off your tuition while I'm gone, contact Gran and Gramps in Boston. They will pay.

I AM sorry but we are both in danger. Your father is capable of murder.

STAY SAFE, Mini-me.

LOVE, Mom

P.S. His little girlfriend ELLA NOVAK bragged about having a picture of your boyfriend's GENITALS. She has been using it to accomplish things for your father. God knows what. I am sick of finding out about his little perversions.

. . .

I READ the email out loud to Crispin and finished with, "See? She's finally lost it."

Crispin seemed to be taking her email seriously. I was torn on the other hand. She could be manipulative when she wanted to be. Daddy was obviously no angel, but Frances was talking recklessly. Crispin moved closer to me, his warmth forcing me to acknowledge how goddamn cold and numb I felt.

"Are you okay?" He asked.

"Yeah. Of course I'm okay. She's being overly dramatic."

"About your father? I wouldn't call it overdramatic," Crispin said, his face growing stern and pensive. He was getting on my nerves instantly. We were done with the drama, therefore this had to be Frances' insanity.

"I don't want to think about this," I said dismissively, stuffing my feelings and hoping I could stuff my mother's words and ignore them.

The most relevant part hit Crispin and he blurted out, "Hang on. Did she say that Ella has a picture of my cock?"

"You're the one who dated her," I snapped in frustration. "Did you send it to her?"

And what about the dick pic and the rape threat? I wondered if Ella's possession of Crispin's dick pic had some connection.

"No! She probably took it when I passed out. I'm not even hard. It makes me look *really* small," Crispin said. Was that seriously what he took issue with here? That his dick didn't look big enough? I glared at Crispin, hoping I could melt him down to a size that would reasonably allow me to give him a Texan ass-whooping.

"That's not what Mandy and Agatha said."

Crispin turned red.

"It's a bit much," he said. "I can't have my cock making the rounds."

"I tried to warn you."

"I didn't think it would spread to America. How the bloody hell did your mum get a hold of it? My cock's infectious!"

"Well, you got rid of the chlamydia, now you just have to stop showing your dick to random women."

"You don't understand. There's no way Ella could have that dick pic. I don't expect you to believe me but... it's like... I just don't think she could have taken it. She's a girl. I would remember her taking a picture of my cock."

"Fine. Maybe you're right. Maybe she did it while you were sleeping."

"Or maybe... it's someone else who's seen my cock," Crispin said. Was he trying to get me more upset? I tried to stick to the thread of our investigation instead of my increasingly unstable feelings about Crispin's traveling dick pic.

"And gave it to Ella?"

"Sure."

"I can't believe I'm saying this but... can you make a list of all the people who have seen your stupid dick?"

"Sure," Crispin said, grinning at me. "But I think it might influence my chances of taking you to bed tonight. So perhaps I'd better get that out of the way first..."

He pressed his lips to my neck and dragged me close to him. I wanted to push him away but I just couldn't. He smelled amazing. His hair was all gross from the gym, but I liked it when he smelled all sweaty and sexy.

"This is torture," I whispered, running my fingers down his back.

Chapter Fifteen

Crispin *totally* distracted me with sex. He was in a freaky mood and he held me in all types of crazy positions, making me cum over and over again. Once I was an exhausted mess, I fell asleep in my bed with Crispin cuddling me. When someone tapped my shoulder, I assumed it was Crispin waking me up.

I grumbled and pulled my blankets over my head when I heard the voice whisper, "Amina!"

"Mandy?"

I pulled my blanket down and squinted. Mandy Desai leaned over, her giant black eyes nearly scaring the crap out of me in the dark.

"What's going on?"

"I know it's late but…"

"Where's Crispin?"

Mandy's lips pursed into a thin line.

"I just got a text from Sarah Clifford. He's in the Dean's Office."

"What?"

"Wake up. I'll bring the other girls in here. You'll need a *lot of support* if he's expelled."

"Expelled?!"

I sat up straight as Mandy scurried out of our room to grab a midnight support team. It was later than midnight. 3:45 a.m.

What trouble could Crispin have possibly found himself in at 3:45 a.m. He hadn't texted me and when I texted him, he didn't reply. Before I could work myself into a full blown panic and call Violet at 3:45 a.m., Mandy returned with other girls from the dorm who had appropriately sympathetic looks on their faces.

Julia, Mandy and Sarah G entered my room. Sarah's blue eyes looked bloodshot and she looked different without her full face of makeup. No one got to see her without her "face" except the girls in the dorm. Mandy held one of my hands and I didn't have the strength to pull it away from her and just tell me what the hell is going on.

Julia blew a wisp of strawberry blond hair out of her face and sighed dramatically.

"I lost Rock Paper Scissors, so I have to tell you... Crispin *stabbed* his roommate. He's nearly been hauled off by the police but for now, he's sitting in the Dean's Office."

"He did WHAT?!"

Mandy offered a friendly squeeze.

"It's okay, Amina. Take all the time you need to process."

"I-I don't need time to process. I have to go over there. I have to find him."

"You *can't* break any more school rules," Mandy said. "We won't let you. We'll sit up all night with you if we must and in the morning, we'll march over and find out the truth."

"Hold on," Sarah said in her gravely voice. "I've got text messages. The tennis group chat has fresh rumors."

"Please be *judicious* in what you share," Mandy said, throwing her a warning look.

Another pale hand pushed my bedroom door open. Violet.

"What are you doing here?"

"Sneaking out, of course," Vi whispered, her face completely red. "My best friend's in trouble. Jack told me that Crispin stabbed Devin."

What the hell? I didn't want to believe it, but how many times had I been there before?

"I know… I can't *believe* he'd do something so stupid. Was there any motive for this?"

"He must have had a good reason," Mandy said, as if there was any good reason for the way Crispin acted. He was just… wild. I couldn't tame that crazy ass white boy if I tried. Now, he'd stabbed Devin. Not when Devin was sleeping with me, but now. Just when I'd trusted him again. My stomach churned.

"Oh shit…" I muttered, as Crispin's possible motive hit me like a bus. He had been musing over who else saw his dick. I assumed he meant a girl, but guys saw each other naked all the time. They lived together too.

"What's wrong?" Julia and Violet said at once, their speaking together made doubly awkward by the fact that they weren't even close.

"Devin leaked his dick pic," I whispered. "That has to be it."

"Gay shit. Nice," Sarah G said, earning her a sharp elbow in the side from Julia.

"Wait… you mean the threatening dick pic?" Mandy said.

I nodded solemnly.

"That's awful. What Devin's done is a *sex crime*. It's revenge porn," she said seriously.

"Isn't revenge porn supposed to be sexy?" I muttered. "He's not even hard."

"Wait... you *knew* it was Crispin's?" Mandy said. "You lied?"

"I didn't mean to... I just... Someone's been sending Crispin's dick pic around with weird stuff attached for a *long* time."

Mandy seemed to calm down once I gave her my reasonable explanation, but I still felt bad for lying in the first place.

"Who wrote the threat then?" Vi pressed.

"I don't know," I muttered groggily. "Lots of people have the pic apparently."

I wiped my eyes and realized I *did* know. I didn't want to tell them about my mom's email. Ella Novak? She was the one who made the threats, but she'd had Devin's help. I made a mental note to give that stupid ginger a good kick in his shriveled hairy nuts. Crispin had gone off the deep end and stabbed Devin so the chances of Ella Novak surviving this information leak were next to zero. Sorry, girl. I tried to save your ass.

"Listen, we'll get through this. Amina? Jack's calling his parents and I've already spoken to Daddy. Crispin won't get in trouble for this. Devin's been a prick for far too long."

"Hasn't he given half the school chlamydia?" Sarah muttered.

"He's done that and worse," Vi said.

"Such a wanker," Mandy added supportively.

Julia gasped and stared at her phone.

"There's already a rumor that the boys are blaming this on the sexual assault awareness campaign and they want the whole thing shut down."

"This has nothing to do with our campaign," Vi said.

"It's just a rumor," Mandy said. "Don't believe it, Amina. The boys are just stupid."

Julia continued announcing updates from her smoking hot group chat.

Her eyes scanned the screen as she said, "Felix Stubbins called Vi a feminazi and apparently Jack Dyson threatened to kick his arse. The football team's divided."

Vi went pale and then hurriedly began typing on her phone.

"You are *not* a feminazi," Mandy said to her reassuringly. Vi gave her a grateful look.

We spent the rest of the night huddled together, waiting for Crispin to text me or waiting for updates from Jack. I didn't want Crispin to go to jail. I barely worried about Devin.

Vi started crying at one point because her brothers and her dad all made fun of her for her feminist beliefs. I didn't even know that about her. Julia let me read all the texts on her phone as she caught a few minutes of sleep in Mandy's bed.

Sarah G's group chat didn't have any updates about Crispin and his alleged crime, but she had plenty of updates about the new hookup gossip. Mandy didn't enjoy hook up gossip. Sarah G laughed at a text on her phone.

"Ella Novak is such a slut. I admire it, really."

"That's so mean," Mandy said.

I didn't admire it, but I also didn't want to talk about Ella.

Forgetting her was the best way for me to move on. I had bigger problems. Keeping quiet didn't stop Sarah G from going on.

"What, it's true? She's allegedly banging some billionaire who is like paying her to dress like a skank," Sarah G said salaciously. Mandy rolled her eyes to indicate her displeasure, but Sarah G didn't appear to give a crap.

Vi and I made awkward eye contact. John Hewett wishes he was a billionaire.

"She's probably lying," Mandy said immediately. "Ella lies about everything. She lied about Amina."

"True," Sarah G said, quickly enough that it was actually relieving.

"I don't want to talk about her," Vi said. "Jack hasn't texted me back in thirty minutes and the last thing he said was that... well... he spelled some of the words wrong but I think he said that there were police officers in their dorm room."

"Are they arresting Crispin!?" I said, hating how panicked I sounded. I'd been doing a good job of holding it together so far. But now, everything was falling apart. Why the hell couldn't Crispin stay out of trouble?

White boy, I told you to stay out of trouble...

Chapter Sixteen

I waited outside the Dean's Office with my spontaneously assembled "L.C. Support Team" the next morning as soon as we were allowed to leave our dorms.

Vi was outside, talking to her father outside his white Rolls Royce. Her dad was really handsome. He looked like a young George Clooney with a smile just like Violet's. Vi was red-faced and screaming at him. I heard the word *chauvinist* as we entered the school house.

I paced back and forth for a while longer outside the Dean's Office. If I sat down, I thought I'd fall asleep and probably never wake up. I was tired and worried about Crispin.

Mandy rubbed my back supportively and Julia handed me a Swedish fish.

"More candy. You need more candy," she said.

I nodded as I continued pacing.

"What's going on in there? Are there any cops?"

"I dare someone to look under the door," Mandy said.

"I'll do it," Sarah G said, eager to get into a push-up position and slowly lower herself to the floor, flexing all her muscles. She whispered as her cheek touched the carpet outside the dean's office, "I can't see anything. There are... several pairs of black shoes and a pair of red high heels."

"That's not helpful," Mandy whispered.

Sarah G pumped out a quick set of ten pushups and then jumped to her feet.

"Well, at least I got a workout in," she says excitedly, flexing her biceps and kissing one of them.

"Sarah, this is an emergency. If her boyfriend gets kicked out of school, that would be like majorly traumatic."

I didn't want to think about what would happen to me and Crispin if he had to drop out of school. Would I stay at Rapetti without him? Would he want to live nearby? Sarah G was already tuning Mandy out and glancing down at her phone.

"Ew! Ella and Felix are planning to hook up," Sarah announced. "I can't believe how many guys she sleeps with. How does she get such good grades?"

Mandy chided, "Sarah, we shouldn't gossip."

"It's not gossip to say they're planning," Sarah said, desperate to defend herself.

"Yes, it is."

Paige rolled her eyes.

"Who cares who Ella or anyone else is sleeping with? The boys at this school suck. All the guys I've slept with here have been like... three inches," Paige said disdainfully. "I can't wait to go back to Edinburgh on holiday. I met a guy there who was six inches. Biggest I've ever had. I thought I'd be getting laid here, not struggling to impress boys who don't wash their pants."

Well, damn. I'm glad Paige had never seen Crispin's dick because she would have clung to him like a howler monkey. I nodded sympathetically to throw her off the trail.

"You know how to impress boys?" Sarah said, then she stuck her tongue into her cheek.

"What does that mean?" Mandy asked.

"It means sucking cock," Paige said. "What, haven't you ever done it?"

"This is stupid," Mandy said. "We should just go in there and—

Before she could finish her sentence, the door to the Dean's office thrust open. Two police officers walked out, but they weren't dragging Crispin along in handcuffs. I heard his deep voice and his posh accent on the other side of the door. Crispin was okay.

"I apologize, Dean Leonard. I've been aggravated by recent personal news regarding my parents. I assure you, it was an unfortunate choice and I will make amends to McLeod."

"Ensure that you do, Mr. Barclay."

"Thank you, Agatha."

"Yes, carry on."

Crispin stormed out of the Dean's office and nearly didn't notice us. Except a gaggle of seven Year 12s didn't exactly scream subtle. He turned to me and muttered, "Fuck…"

"She's been worried sick about you!" Mandy said.

The girls stared at him. Crispin gave us all an apologetic look and then his magnetic blue eyes fixed on me. His gaze was like a spotlight. Everything around me vanished and there was just *him*. My 6'6" giant, fiercely prepared to protect me.

"I'm sorry," Crispin said to all of us gently. "Amina? Will you come? We can talk. Thanks for keeping her company, ladies."

"Hope you're okay, Crispin," Julia said softly. The girls mumbled other soft words that I couldn't make sense of. I was too angry with Crispin to allow him to take my hand when he reached for it, and I followed him out of the school building both outraged and perplexed.

"You *stabbed* Devin."

"You shouldn't believe everything you hear," Crispin huffed.

"Okay," I said. "So what happened?"

"I stabbed Devin."

"Crispin!"

"Sorry. I know. I'm probably dumped again."

I ignored his little comment.

"White boy, why?!"

"Because he took the photo of my cock after football practice and gave it to Ella Novak," Crispin said. "I finally pieced it together. He's a cunt who will do just about anything to get his cock wet and he shagged my girlfriend last semester, treating her like shit. I'd stab him again if I got the chance. Thankfully, I'm getting a medical single. No more roommates. No more bloody Devin. It ought to be peaceful."

Crispin seemed unconcerned about anything except his housing situation. As far as he was concerned, he'd solved everything, and there were no further problems. *Mind blowing.*

"Is he going to die!?"

133

"I said I stabbed him... not that I killed him. It's a flesh wound. He'll be fine."

"Crispin, you could go to jail."

"He's not pressing charges. Listen, Lips, with everything that's gone on in my life, people understand that I'm on edge."

"You're saying you need to stab people to cope?"

What kind of white people mental health was this?

Crispin shrugged and then he stopped walking. He put his hand on my hips which felt incredibly nice. Then he pressed his forehead to mine.

"I lost control. He mentioned shagging you. He talked about you like you were meat. I am so sensitive when it comes to you..."

Then he kissed me and I allowed his Lips to part mine. Oh, Crispin, why can't I ever stay away from you? Once we'd finished a deep, slow kiss, Crispin murmured, "I'm skipping class today and if you skip with me... I'll take the blame and help with all your make up work."

"I can't just skip."

"I'll call Dean Leonard myself."

"Fine. Okay. I'll skip."

"Good. We've got our presentation tonight, anyway. I need to practice my speech. I realized... I'm the victim of campus sexual harassment. Revenge porn."

"You didn't even care about it at first," I pointed out. We kept walking around the building together, not straying too far but staying far enough away we could have some privacy. The countryside ambience almost always seemed ironic considering the nonstop drama at our college.

Crispin sighed and shrugged again. "I didn't realize some

sick freak would use my cock to threaten people. I mean… my cock is not threatening at all."

"It's like the size of my forearm," I pointed out, ducking as a large bird attempted to dive bomb my hair.

The scent of freshly cut grass was calming, but not doing enough to calm me down entirely.

Crispin kept going on about his dick. "That's a bit big but surely it's just… you know… average? Except my team. They're pretty small."

"I don't want to know *why* you see each other's dicks."

"Shit happens. Sometimes, your dick hangs out."

"Ew. Just ew," I grumbled.

"Come on, Twiggy. Let's get out of here and get some sleep. And by sleep, I mean I grovel and apologize for stabbing your ex."

There it was. A twinge of remorse. Unfortunately, he had to say something gross right there in the same sentence.

"Don't call Devin my ex," I said. "It makes me feel seriously gross."

Crispin chuckled and kissed my cheek.

"Fine. I ought to get your friends flowers. I also ought to learn their names. Just… don't introduce any of them to Kaito."

"Why do you hang out with that freak?"

"He's not so bad," Crispin said. "Just weird and violent. And Japanese."

"Something about that sounds off," I muttered.

Crispin shrugged and put a cigarette between his teeth.

"Ready for a drive, babe?" he asked, walking closer to me as he patted down his pockets for a lighter.

"I'm ready for a nap," I said with a yan.

"Perfect," Crispin whispered. "I can help with that. Let the car purr you to sleep."

We drove to the cottage and I fell asleep as soon as the engine started. Crispin had parked and waited a few minutes for me to wake up on my own. I yawned and unraveled my limbs. Crispin leaned over and kissed my cheek.

"Twiggy. You sleep like an angel…"

"Is the front door ajar?" I muttered, staring ahead.

We were snapped out of our romantic moment and we both tumbled sleepily out of the cur. The front door had been only slightly ajar, but Crispin was still worried. He stormed in, all panicked, but when we wandered inside, the cottage was bare. Not like it had been robbed, but like it had been deep-cleaned and nobody had lived there in ages. There was a small folded letter on the table.

Crispin called out, "Freddie! Katrina!"

But I didn't bother calling for them. I made a beeline for the letter and absorbed each word.

Chapter Seventeen

Dear Crispin,
We've gone away for a while.
Katrina's withdrawn from Rapetti.
Love, Freddie & Katrina

P.S. Don't be angry. I won't get caught. —F

U nderneath that, Katrina had scrawled, "Freddie wrote that, I do not love you except in the Christian way."

"Is this a bloody joke?" Crispin snarled, snatching the note out of my hand and then screaming their names loudly, as if that would make his sister and my wayward Bible thumping friend materialize.

"Katrina's *withdrawn* from school? Has she told Vi? She

never even mentioned this," I said. I wondered if Katrina's parents knew about her pregnancy yet. They would have to find out eventually and from what I knew about them, they wouldn't react well.

Crispin murmured, "Does Katrina ever make sense? Freddie probably put her up to this."

"We should call them."

"Fuck!" He snapped.

"Hey. Calm down. We can just call them and convince them to tell us where they are."

Crispin groaned.

"I don't want to do any of it."

He turned to me and crumpled the note, throwing it across the room.

"Fuck it. If they want to run, I'll let them run. They can't run far without me. Freddie uses my card."

I didn't bother point out that Katrina had access to her own money.

"Are you sure that's a good idea?"

"No. It's probably bloody stupid. But I have you here and you're mine again, so I'd rather not worry about my sister and my pregnant sort-of-sister-in-law."

Crispin could be painfully disinterested in anything that didn't directly affect him and I could detect his apathy about the note despite the surprising nature of the situation. I wanted to pinch his ass and bring him back into reality. This was important.

"Katrina's not your sister-in-law."

"Yes. But she's my niece or nephew's mother as much as it pains me."

"Okay. So Katrina's gone. That's it..." I said, folding my

arms and giving Crispin another opportunity to have a real emotional response. I was down to investigate, but considering how rigid her was about not giving a crap, I wasn't sure I had a partner in crime.

"We'll worry about them later. I just want you here," Crispin said.

So really, he didn't give a shit about the note. I rolled my eyes.

"I want to call Vi and see if she knows," I said.

Crispin sighed with frustration. "She probably does. Don't call her. Just... let's make sure they aren't hiding in the bedrooms."

This was his idea of compromise, so I gave up arguing with him. I followed Crispin around checking the bedrooms. All signs of Freddie and Katrina disappeared.

We stopped at the room Freddie had been occupying and Crispin picked up a picture of their family. They were in Barbados. Crispin had awkwardly long limbs and freckles. Freddie glared straight ahead. Crispin's father looked exactly like him with blue eyes boring into the camera. I shuddered just looking at the picture.

Crispin's thumb brushed over his father's face and he murmured, "I promised I'd be different from him. I'm not doing a particularly good job."

"What was he like?"

Crispin knew what John Hewett was like. I wanted to know about his father.

"He was never there. I always had my mum... but not him. He was cold. Distant. Cruel. Just like August."

Crispin paused for a moment and then murmured, "And he was very old."

I moved closer to Crispin and he pulled me close to him as soon as he could. He kissed the top of my head and whispered, "I never want to be a monster."

I wrapped my arms around him and pulled my big muscular white boy against me.

"I get why you want to protect people," I whispered. "I really get it."

"I couldn't do it for any of them. Not for my mum. Not for Freddie. I just want one person... one person."

He kissed me hard again and then pulled away, his cheeks darkened into a blush hue. We walked back into the hallway together, staring at each other. I didn't mind when Crispin looked at me because then I could really take my time staring at him.

"I'd very much like to take you to bed now," he said in a soft, polite voice.

"What's stopping you?"

"Trousers. Your bra. The fact that if I do the wrong thing... you'll dump me again."

He looked both sad and insecure, emotional states completely uncommon in Crispin. I held him close to me, wanting to reassure him and wanting him to reassure me just as much with his warmth and presence. His chest moved in time with his heartbeat, causing warmth and pleasure to spread through me as I held him against me.

"I won't dump you," I promised him, wanting to mean it.

"Right," Crispin said, stroking the stubble on his chin pensively. Uncertainty colored his pink face. His brows scrunched up again, and I wanted to kiss the tip of his nose. And all over him. My emotions towards him were all over the place, but I mostly wanted him close. That part was consistent.

Again, he looked like he hadn't been sleeping. He stared at me for a few moments and then he blurted out. "I really love you."

"I love you too."

He paused for a moment and that pensive, uncertain expression returned. He wasn't thinking about Freddie or Katrina, but he *was* thinking about something. I squeezed him tightly, as if that could coax it out of him. Surprisingly, Crispin shifted a little and started to speak, exposing the dark thoughts that occupied the back of his mind.

"I don't know what I'll have to do to get that little black book."

Shit. That. He was right it was more important than finding Katrina and Freddie, who could mostly handle themselves.

"Hopefully, you'll just have to ask John," I said, trying to keep things as light-hearted as possible. I could tell Crispin wanted to get serious. He pulled me tightly against him and my heart felt all warm and fluttery. I let myself sink into his chest and he gruffly squeezed me.

"I won't hurt you again, babe," he murmured. "I won't let myself. I'll set you free if that's what I have to do."

"Don't say that," I whispered. "I tried that stupid little break up. It sucked."

"Finally, you admit it."

"Hush, white boy."

We wandered out into the kitchen from the hallway, and Crispin lifted me onto the counter and spread my legs, stepping between them and placing his firm hands on my thighs.

"I can hush," he whispered. "If that's what you want. But I'd rather make this cottage loud."

We had done it almost everywhere in the cottage, but there was something particularly naughty about having my legs spread on the kitchen counter. Crispin didn't care. He was down to have sex just about anywhere.

"Even before having a cup of tea?" I teased.

"Definitely," he whispered, grabbing my hips and pulling me closer. I wrapped my thighs around his torso. His eyes flickered with desire as I drew him closer to me. He loved whenever I showed him any signs of my organic need for him.

"I miss you," he said.

"Do you just mean the sex part?" I whispered, mostly because of the way Crispin's hands touched my thighs, but also because of the way our push and pull dynamic had me rubbed raw. I was as uncertain as he was, but ready to stumble back towards him after the pain of separation.

I didn't want to be away from Crispin again, but I also didn't want him to hurt me because I didn't know how much more I could take. I needed him to be all in with all parts of me.

"Of course not," Crispin said, only mildly offended, "I miss everything about you when I don't have you. I'm crazy about you, Twiggy."

He grabbed my cheeks and kissed me again. It was easy to believe Crispin loved me when he kissed me. He was so warm and he kissed with such soft, gentle, precision, it was like he truly did love me.

"Devin…" I whispered.

"Please don't call out his name when I'm hard for you," Crispin murmured.

"I'm not calling out his name. You stabbed him. I want to know if... you're okay."

"He violated me. He violated you. He deserved it. The only reason Ella's alive is because you have a soft spot for her."

"According to Sarah G, she's hooking up with someone else. Felix Stubbins?"

Crispin snorted and rolled his eyes.

"I'm sure she is."

"What do you mean by that?"

"Listen, Amina... I don't want to think about the rubbish at school. I have you here and this is what I want. My woman. My cottage. My bed."

He bent his head to his neck and gave me a different kiss. Crispin kissed like this when he wanted us naked. He had an insatiable sex drive that burned slowly, heating up with kisses and oral before repeated lovemaking. It wasn't really ritualistic or boring. He just kissed me and watched how I responded, and then he somehow knew exactly what I liked.

Turning me on got him *really* hard. He always came hardest after he made me finish. Remembering that made me drag him closer by his collar. Crispin chuckled and murmured, "I'm yours, Lips. Forever. Always. Yours."

I reached for his belt buckle and pulled his dick out. Crispin chuckled and bit down on his lower lip.

"What are your plans for that?"

"The girls were saying earlier that blowjobs are the best way to impress a guy. You never ask for them. If you don't get it from me, maybe you'll get it somewhere else."

Crispin put his hand on mine, closing my grasp around his cock. His jaw clenched as he moved his hips and then his dick forward in my grasp. It was like a part of him enjoyed this slow torment.

"Amina, sweetheart. I don't need you to impress me. I'm the man. I'm the one who has to impress you."

"Right. Like you aren't just going to get it from other girls."

Crispin looked hurt.

"Sex doesn't work like that, Twiggy. Sex isn't about taking and impressing or about forcing women to act out a pornographic drama. It's about your body. Your cunt. And what feels right for both of us."

Ugh. He was always so dramatic. I loved it.

"Damn, white boy."

"I'm serious," he whispered, gliding his hips forward again and sliding the smooth shaft of his cock through my grasp. He groaned and leaned his forehead against mine. He took my lower lip in his and then pulled away for a moment.

"See this? You touching me softly, with no force on my part. It's natural and it feels more amazing than any blowjob to have you… appreciating me."

"How do you always know the right things to say?"

Crispin smirked.

"That can't possibly be true or I wouldn't get dumped as often as I do."

"Shut up."

He slid his hips forward again and I grabbed the base of his cock, holding him close to me as I kissed him. He chuckled and kissed my neck.

Crispin murmured into my ear, "Sweetheart, I can't stop myself. I want to take you now."

"Rip my clothes off," I gasped desperately, giving Crispin an outlet for his aggression and darkness. I didn't know if he would take the opportunity.

His eyes roved over my clothing and over my body. I couldn't tell if he was hesitating or planning. Then he smirked and right away, I knew. I never should have doubted. Crispin would never pass up an opportunity to rip my clothes off. He loved stripping me naked, unwrapping me like a present, or roughly ripping fabric away from my flesh, depending on his appetite.

Tonight was urgent. He ran his hands over my clothes, finding the weakest spot with precision he shouldn't have had and then he ripped everything off with his firm grasp, taking the clothes off piece by piece. I gasped in surprise as he clutched my bare body to his. He was agitated with desire now, his cock visibly hard, and I needed him badly after such a raw display of his aggression and power.

He pressed his hand to my bare crotch and groaned.

"You're so wet, babe. I love it…"

Crispin pried his fingers out from between my legs and sucked on them. A lot. He closed his eyes and sighed like he was savoring a truly spectacular fruit juice and not just whatever had been gushing around between my legs since he started kissing me.

"Screw everyone else," he murmured. "I just want you to be happy, babe."

He ripped his shirt off and graced me with his incredible abs. Even off the field, Crispin kept his body chiseled. He made it seem effortless. My mouth watered as I scraped my fingers down his washboard abs. He chuckled and pulled me close.

"Come here, you little beast," he whispered. "Give me a kiss."

I eagerly gave him a kiss and scooted to the edge of the counter. We didn't bother with protection. Crispin pressed the head of his dick against my entrance and this time, he felt enormous. It was like having an apple pressed against my crotch. The immediate pressure of his head moving between my lips sent a surge of pleasure through me. I clung to Crispin's biceps.

"Am I hurting you, babe?"

"No."

"Good," he whispered. "You feel nice. Really tight."

He moved a little deeper inside me. I clutched his biceps harder. A tight knot of pleasure in the base of my stomach spread throughout my thighs as my body anticipated the certain pleasure of accepting Crispin Barclay between my legs. He clutched the base of my spine and pulled me close to him so that his cock was buried properly between my legs.

I cried out as our bodies joined and the immensity of his shaft pulsing between my legs filled me with a rush of pain and pleasure intermingled. He moved deeper between my legs, his icy eyes fixed on me. He moved his hand between my legs and found my clit instantly. I moaned as he rubbed me slowly, keeping his cock still.

"Oh yeah…" I whispered.

"Like that, babe?"

"Yes…"

"I love your pretty black pussy…"

I whimpered and bucked my hips to show my satisfaction

with him. The gush between my legs only made me move with less control as I twisted my hips and pulled his dick inside me as deeply as I could take him.

He grunted and repeated those six spicy words, provoking another untamed gush between my legs. I'd never heard Crispin say anything crazy like that. I grabbed onto his back and moved my hips forward, moaning loudly as his hands and dick made me feel *so* good.

"Oh yes," he whispered. "I can feel you get really wet when I talk about your black pussy…"

"Crispin…" I whispered, planning to tell him off about it.

Instead, he whispered in my ear, "I wish I could cum inside your black pussy with my big white cock."

"I need you," I gasped, holding onto him, feeling his body against mine and craving even more of him than ever before. My nails dug into him, encouraging Crispin to take me harder.

He moved his hips into me faster and with his hands on my clit, I came hard. Really hard. Crispin kept moving his hips but he didn't say anything dirty anymore. He kissed me and moved slowly between my legs, making love to me until I came again. He pulled out of me and then flipped me around so I faced away from him.

"Do you?"

"Yes," I gasped. "Cum inside me…"

He leaned forward, pressing his muscular body against mine as he cupped my ass and whispered in my ear, "I'd like to enter your tight cunt from behind."

"Yes…" I whispered.

The large head of Crispin's dick pressed against my entrance again. This angle felt like it would be hard to get him in. We had such a massive height difference that Crispin had to lift me and he grabbed my hips with one hand to get me to the perfect height so he could slide into me. We both groaned as he entered me.

"Fuck, your arse is gorgeous," He moaned as he pumped his hips furiously. If he'd had any control before, he lost it. He held me against him, pleasuring my body with kisses and making me cum with his hand as he thrust into me from behind. He was getting close after that.

"I love your arse," he murmured, kissing my neck as he came. His cock spurting cum into me made me cum again because he just felt so damned good. I leaned against the counter, panting for breath until Crispin lifted me over his shoulder and carried me triumphantly back to his bedroom for more.

Chapter Eighteen

Crispin licked the last dollop of whipped cream off my neck. I shivered as his tongue explored my flesh and then he sucked on it, making sure my neck was clean as I leaned into his protective grasp. *Damn.*

"There," he whispered, "I think I got it all."

"How did you eat three cans of whipped cream?" I said, shivering as I allowed him to hold my body tightly against his. We had damn near destroyed the kitchen with the sheer number of positions we tried out. I was sore everywhere and Crispin had a completely unhinged look in his eye.

"You're tasty, babe," he answered. "I told you I wanted to lick you from head to toe."

"This is disturbing," I gasped, ignoring my nipples stiffening wickedly.

"Disturbing? That you came four times while I licked whipped cream off you? I think it's disturbing that you aren't more appreciative. Perhaps I ought to tie you up and teach you some gratitude."

I giggled and ran my hands over Crispin's jawline. His

face gave way to a smile. He'd been smiling more since we got back together. I liked his smile. It softened the giant blond beast and I could almost see a sweet little boy behind his eyes.

"I have to admit, sweetheart. Freddie and Katrina ought to worry me. I don't know where or why they could have gone. And if you're worried… I'm worried."

I liked that he was taking my emotions seriously.

I asked, "Do you trust them?"

"Freddie… yes. But not Katrina. And I don't trust Freddie with August's baby. I'll have to track them down eventually. No rush when I've got an angel in my bed…"

Crispin dove into me again, licking and kissing me. Then we both desperately needed a shower and he made love to me in the gigantic claw foot tub. We were both exhausted and it was nearly dawn when we were finished. I didn't want to stop clinging to Crispin and I didn't have to. I wrapped my arms around his neck and got straight into bed with him. In the morning, Crispin woke me up with gentle kisses.

"Sexual assault," he whispered into my ear.

"Huh?"

"The campaign?" He murmured. "Remember our encore performance?"

"Okay. Couldn't you have chosen something romantic to whisper?"

"Sorry," he mumbled, clamping his arms down around me and squeezing me like a teddy bear. "Sorry for everything."

I tried to free myself from Crispin's bear-like grasp, but nothing would work to get him off me.

"Barclay!"

"You're mine, Twiggy. I'm not letting you go."

"You're crushing me!"

"Yes…" he murmured. "Crushing you with my love…"

"Boy, bye!"

"No… hello…"

He kissed me and cuddled me a bit longer and then Crispin made me breakfast. This morning, he was in a great mood but he wasn't hungry. Yeah, white boy, binge eating whipped cream will do that to you. He made me some oatmeal with cinnamon, brown sugar and french toast on the side. When I complained it was too much, he ate a single bite of my oatmeal and then watched me eat the entire thing.

Once I finished, he only said one thing.

"Freddie stopped eating when we were thirteen. She nearly died and they sent her to hospital again. I always cried when she left. She doesn't know. If she did, she'd probably laugh. But… I don't want to lose you. Not like that."

I let him wrap me up in another embrace. His protectiveness made me want to do better. It always had. Half the reason I started eating was to make Crispin happy. Now, I ate for myself more often than not. But his caring made all the difference. I wanted to try.

We drove back to campus together. Crispin put on Meg Thee Stallion and we were rapping along, having a great time. We were almost late to class, but it was worth it. I barely had time to get my uniform on.

Vi, Sarah Clifford, Jack and Mandy were all eager for our meeting after school. The entire school was looking forward to our presentation and campaign, so this final meeting was crucial to getting everything ready for our big night. I was five minutes late and Crispin was a few seconds behind, power-walking to try to catch up to me.

"Were you two just shagging?" Mandy teased.

"Not this time," Crispin said, with a wink, earning a sharp elbow in his side from me.

Vi glared at him.

"You're late."

"So is Amina."

"Don't tattle on her," Vi said. "Amina's not late. A lady's never late."

"Thank you, Violet. Always having my back," I said, sticking my tongue out at Crispin.

Jack Dyson groaned and yawned slowly like a sloth waking up from a long nap. It finally hit me who Jack sounded like. David Attenborough. It was weird to hear an elderly British man's voice coming from a giant hairy football player, but that's exactly who he sounded like.

"Vi, babe. I think I made a typo on the flyer."

"Again?" Vi said through gritted teeth.

"Listen, Bainbridge," Crispin said. "Can you review my speech? I edited it more."

Violet snatched Crispin's paper.

"Your handwriting is surprisingly neat," Vi commented.

"Thanks. Four years of penmanship camp."

"Sounds like the most boring thing ever," Jack said, biting into a tangerine and then spitting out the skin. Mandy made a disgusted look on her face and moved the tangerine skin off her notebook.

"Shut up, Dyson," Crispin grumbled.

Jack shrugged and plopped the rest of the orange in his mouth, giving up on spitting on the skin and just muddling through the chewing.

"So... Devin called me earlier," Jack said as the orange bobbed around his open mouth. "He's a wanker."

"Right," Crispin said, growing uncomfortable.

"Can we stay on topic, please?" Vi snapped. "Crispin, this looks great."

"Are you sure? It's not too... wordy?"

"I mean, there are words, sure. But it's not overly long."

"Cool. Thanks."

"This is really good, Crispin. People will actually listen to you. I'm impressed."

Crispin's cheeks turned red. He took the paper back from her as Jack chewed on his orange.

"Why can't I make a speech?" Jack said.

No one wanted to answer and we all glanced off in different directions mumbling nonsense. Finally, Mandy broke the silence. She sat up straight with an excited smile.

"The t-shirts are here. I'll go pick them up."

"I'll help," Jack offered.

Mandy offered Vi a sympathetic look and she waved them both off. Crispin tapped his pencil on the table.

"Violet. Do you mind if I ask you a personal question?"

"What kind of question?" Vi retorted.

Yeah, white boy. Huh? Vi gave Crispin a suspicious look.

"Do you really think Dyson's good enough for you?"

Vi glanced down at her phone hurriedly.

"He tries *really* hard."

"Right. Well. If you ever need me to beat him up, let me know. If you're Amina's friend I just want you to know... I'll look out for you."

"Thanks, Crispin," Vi said. "That's sweet."

"Right."

153

"Just don't ever stab him, okay?"

"Oh no, I only reserve the right to stab gingers."

Vi giggled. Wow. This was the first conversation they'd had without massive glaring.

"Have you heard from Katrina?" Vi asked me. "She's withdrawn. I can't believe it. She won't give me any explanation at all. She says she's coming back next semester but I don't know how she's going to get on with her divinity school applications."

Before I could answer, Mandy scurried around the corner, carrying a giant box overflowing with blue and pink t-shirts.

"Get Consent!" Mandy squealed. "These designs are perfect!"

"Thank you very much," I said excitedly.

I hadn't changed out of my uniform and Crispin put his hand on my thigh.

"My girl's a talented artist," Crispin said admiring my t-shirt designs. "I'm really proud of her."

"Aww!!" Mandy said. "Okay, which ones are you going to pick?"

We spread the shirts out on the table and each picked one. We were selling them after our presentation to raise money for a nearby women's shelter. Jack Dyson trailed Mandy by a few minutes with three more boxes tucked underneath his arm. He was already wearing two of the shirts over each other.

"Babe!" He bellowed across the library. "Women Are Not Objects!"

He pulled the door open to our group meeting room and shut it behind him.

"You don't have to scream down the library," Vi muttered.

Jack Dyson was too excited to hold himself back. He wiped some of the juices from his tangerine on his new orange shirt as he excitedly told Vi, "Babe, these shirts are incredible."

"Where's Sarah?" Mandy asked. "She's really late. That's not like her."

"Great point. Where is she?" Vi said, glancing down at her phone.

It wasn't like Sarah Clifford to be late. We had to carry on the meeting without her. Practice, planning and chatting all proceeded nicely. It felt good to be a part of something. Five minutes before the end of the meeting, Sarah Clifford finally burst through the door.

"Oh my God. You wouldn't *believe* where I've been."

"You're about two hours late."

"I know," Sarah said. "But trust me, you all will want to hear this."

Chapter Nineteen

We gathered around patiently to hear Sarah's new information. She had her lips pursed and a very serious expression on her face like the discovery was gravely serious. My heart nervously pattered around my chest, making it hard to think straight while I waited impatiently for Sarah to spit it out.

"Ella Novak's parents are arranging a marriage for her and sending her to Thornwood Academy," Sarah blurted out, nodding excitedly as we all sat there staring at her and looking stupid.

Thornwood Academy was one of our rival schools in the English boarding college system. The school was known for housing England's richest juvenile delinquents. Not just college students who couldn't stay enrolled at other boarding schools, but students who had committed actual crimes.

It was hard to imagine Ella as little more than an inmate... without smiling internally. I tried to keep my emotions to myself and keep a straight face. But I couldn't lie to myself about being happy that Ella was gone. The arranged marriage thing didn't even register at first until Mandy replied. She had been hemming for a while over Sarah's news.

Mandy scrunched her face up and flicked her ponytail of thick black hair over her shoulder. "The arranged marriage bit can't possibly be true."

I didn't want to be racist or anything, but wasn't Mandy an expert on arranged marriages? She had definitely mentioned them a couple times in the past...

"Listen, I got this information from Trevor. He's like her best friend," Sarah said with frustration at receiving any push back.

"Trevor is nobody's best friend..." Vi grumbled.

"I don't get it," Jack said slowly. "I thought only people from Pakistan arranged marriages. Isn't that true Mandeep?"

"I'm from London," Mandy said.

"Right. But originally, you're from... Pakistan? Perhaps, Sri Lanka?"

"Stop. Guessing," Vi hissed, her cheeks turning red.

"Jack, perhaps we ought to focus," Sarah said, upset that Jack's racist comments might ruin the mood. She cleared her throat to take control of the conversational dynamic again.

"Hello, I'm updating you all on Ella Novak. She's leaving the school. Forever. Her parents found out about the whole rich guy she was dating and they're livid. Trevor doesn't know who it is. No one knows. But he turned her blond and everything. It's wicked."

I wanted to ask how Ella had possibly hidden spending her entire Christmas vacation with her rich boyfriend, but I was an expert at hiding things from my parents like most rich kids, so maybe there wasn't anything to that.

"Trevor also makes things up," I pointed out, just in case there was a point there..

I couldn't be so lucky to have Ella Novak leave without it becoming an international incident that Crispin was somehow responsible for, could I? Sarah shrugged, as if to say Trevor was a perfectly acceptable source of information.

I exchanged nervous glances with Crispin who gave me a knowing look but didn't appear to be worried. I knew he would be there for me if this gossip session took a wrong turn.

"How soon is she leaving?" Crispin asked. That was the same question I'd wanted to ask.

"Tonight," Sarah Clifford said. "She's leaving before our campaign. And considering the rumors she's spread, she needs the campaign more than anyone."

Crispin scoffed. "Well, you've certainly changed from last semester."

"So have you," Sarah snapped. "We're in college. We're allowed to change."

"As long as we change for the better, I suppose," Crispin said coolly, without looking at her.

Sarah shot him a glare but then removed her headband and replaced it.

"Yes. I suppose," she said snootily, turning her nose up at Crispin and turning her attention back to the rest of the table. "Either way, Ella's gone. No one knows what happened but her parents think she was completely brainwashed. That's why she's blond now, Trevor says. He doesn't agree with this sugar daddy thing."

"Brainwashed?" Jack said disbelievingly. "Doesn't that like... require a cult leader or something..."

Sarah shrugged. "I just thought she wanted to look like me. She goes for all the guys I like."

Ah, Sarah. Not *all* of them. Maybe Crispin, but the one thing I could say for sure about Sarah Cifford was that she definitely was not attracted to John Hewett.

"I've sworn off boys for a while. My only boys are my stallions," Sarah said, making it a point not to look at Crispin.

"Stallions?" Mandy asked curiously, more interested in the idea of animals than gossip.

"After last semester, I got diagnosed with depression. Mummy got me another emotional support stallion."

"That's sweet."

Sarah nodded approvingly.

"Well, Ella's gone. Good riddance," Vi said. "Let's get back to work. I don't want to think about her."

Sarah shrugged noncommittal, "Neither do I, really. But allegedly, her parents might sue the school for allowing her to enter the relationship since *allegedly*, it all began here. Who knows. It's a pity she'd miss classes."

Vi scoffed and rolled her eyes.

"They won't sue the school," Vi said. "The Novaks are broke. Thomas has her brother Jesse staying with us for a while in Scotland."

Jack's ears perked up.

"Broke? Like... they've run out of millions? How is that possible? Can't they just ask their accountants for more?"

"We should stay on topic," Mandy said assertively.

Sarah shrugged. Mandy pulled out her notebook and managed to get us all back on topic with significant wrestling. We spent the rest of the evening making our last minute preparations. Crispin was the last one to contribute

159

anything and I was almost worried he hadn't given it his best until he practiced the speech, and it was pretty good.

He wanted to draw attention to what male allies could do to support their female friends and classmates. It was just cool that he was down to participate in something like that.

He was so shy, but when he chose to speak out about something, people listened. Sarah's face was red throughout Crispin's entire practice run. Mandy waited for him to finish before she clapped dramatically.

"Well done. I think this will make a huge impact," Mandy said.

"Thanks," Crispin muttered awkwardly.

"Listen, Amina," Sarah said. "Can we talk after this? It's not about tomorrow."

Crispin scowled at her and then glanced at me as if he were my attack dog waiting in the wings. By now, I could handle Sarah. Crispin had nothing to defend me from, so I threw him a sharp glare, hoping that would calm his ass down. He kept a cool interest in the conversation.

"Okay," I said calmly. "What's it about?"

My tone did nothing to hide my distrust. I liked Sarah, and I wanted to move on from our past, but there was still a part of me that didn't trust anyone, and moved cautiously around all information that could be related to Ella or my dad's activities with her. Sarah confirmed my worst suspicions with her response.

"It's about Ella... and... something Trevor told me."

"If there's anything you have to say to me, you can say it to Crispin."

I could tell Sarah wanted to protest, but maybe she didn't feel she had the right to do so.

"Fine," She said. We finished up the meeting together and then Sarah stayed behind with me and Crispin to give me her big news. Crispin was already upset, even if nothing had happened. He was so damn glum when he said goodbye to everyone because of the weight on his mind. I could feel the nervous energy between us, but I was a lot better at hiding my feelings.

Vi and Jack walked off arguing with each other as Mandy called for them to wait up. Crispin put his arm over my shoulder and I waited patiently for Sarah Clifford to say what she wanted to.

"It's just… you ought to be careful. Ella's going through a really hard time and… I don't know how you're involved but Trevor said she had it out for you."

"Amina doesn't have to worry about Ella," Crispin said.

Sarah's lower lip trembled momentarily. She did her best to cover up the involuntary movement.

"You always were *so* protective of her. Even when we were dating. I don't suppose you care how it feels."

Crispin stared at her dumb-founded.

"I—I…"

"You loved her. I get it. But you treated me like rubbish. I regret the way I treated Amina but you don't have an excuse for how you treated me."

Sarah stormed off angrily. Crispin's cheeks were red and he raked his fingers through his hair, lowering his hoodie and mussing his hair in frustration.

"Bloody hell," he grumbled.

"Don't mind Sarah."

"No," Crispin said. "She's right. I was… a bit of a prick."

"Sarah was an asshole last semester too. She said herself that people change."

"I know. But… I ought to have been a bit better about the whole wanting another girl thing."

"What do you mean?"

"I told her I loved another girl. Then I basically wrote an entire English essay about you and made her edit it," Crispin confessed, with shockingly little remorse.

"You did *what*?"

Crispin shrugged.

"What was in the essay?"

"I dunno. Stuff about tits. Stuff about knives. Our teachers encourage me to explore my past. I just… don't see the point."

He stuffed his hands in his pockets and walked me back to my dorm.

"I'd love to come in but I need rest before my big speech," Crispin said, the corners of his lips tugging into a gentle smile.

"It sounds really good."

"I'm sure I'll muck it all up," he said. "I've never been good with crowds. Attention. Whatever."

"You'll be fine. I'll be right there next to you. Holding you down."

"Oh yeah? Are *you* going to talk about your responsibility as a man to stand against sexual assault?"

"No. I was thinking I'd booty pop a few times and distract the crowd while you made a hasty getaway."

"Ah. I see. I'd love to see some of your moves now."

"No way, white boy."

Crispin's eyes gleamed as he pulled me close to him. Our

hips nestled together and I felt this ache… He kissed me and I realized it would be our last one for the night. I missed having him in my bed and tonight, I really wanted him there. Crispin was the perfect cuddle buddy, especially because of his size. It was like laying up next to a cuddly horse and I was living for it.

"Tomorrow," he whispered, kissing me goodnight again.

In the morning, I couldn't wait… First, We sold t-shirts in the dining hall at breakfast and made a killing. Rapetti kids had money to burn and they were ready to support the latest trendy cause. I mean, we had Crispin and Jack Dyson behind a table and they attracted a *lot* of attention, even from Year 13 girls.

Misaki leaned over the table and attempted to flirt with Crispin for a few moments while I was standing right there. He tried to be as boring as possible and then Vi rescued both of us with a terse, "May I help you, Misaki? It's just, I can see Kaito would really like to speak with Crispin."

"Oh, absolutely, Bainbridge. You can help me understand why Year 12s haven't learned to keep their mouths shut yet."

About what?

While Violet turned purple, Misaki stormed away. Crispin's shoulders relaxed.

"I was about to tell her off," he said huffily.

Vi glared at him.

"That's your ex-girlfriend?"

"I was in a dark place."

"I think you were," Vi said haughtily and then stormed off. Crispin groaned and swatted his forehead.

"I keep mucking it up with your friends," he grumbled. "I'm really trying."

Unfortunately for both of us, Vi hadn't just been making things up when she'd said that Kaito Cammish had been approaching our table. Half-Scottish, Half-Japanese, 100% asshole. I didn't see it for Crispin and his creep ass friend.

Kaito nodded at Crispin and then glanced at our informational pamphlets.

"What's up, mate? What's all this about?"

"Feminism," Crispin said.

I elbowed him. That was *not* our explanation speech. I explained our mission as rehearsed for weeks beforehand. *Raising awareness of what constitutes sexual assault, how men can avoid predatory behavior and the best ways women can defend themselves and report such behavior to the administration.*

Kaito looked completely bored.

"Right," Kaito said, glancing from me to Crispin. "Well, I'm having a party before Easter break."

He handed Crispin a gold key.

"Bring tits."

Before Crispin could speak up, or I could say anything, Kaito winked at me and walked away. Mandy heard our entire conversation and came over to me.

"The nerve of him! Crispin, what is his problem?"

Crispin shrugged.

"He's troubled."

"I suspect he is," Mandy sniffed. We didn't have too much time to dwell on Kaito's irritating presence. More of our peers wanted to hear more and by the time breakfast was over, we'd barely eaten, but we'd sold all our t-shirts and stickers.

"We should start doing pre-orders next," Jack Dyson said, a surprisingly genius plan. We didn't know if we were allowed to do that, but Vi set about texting Dean Leonard for permission and we split off to go to class. Our *all-school presentation* was officially mandatory. According to Trevor, our school's headmaster would actually make an appearance. No offense, but our headmaster was seriously old. He could hardly walk anywhere at all and he was mostly a figurehead. The thought of talking about sexual assault in front of this pre-boomer scared the hell out of me.

Crispin was taking it hard. He texted me at 10 a.m.

CRISPIN: I can't talk in front of people. I'm too tall.

    Me: You will kill it boo xx

    Crispin: we can run away together.

    Me: don't think so

    Crispin: grr

Chapter Twenty

We didn't have a class together until after lunch. I had lunch with Vi Bainbridge and Jack Dyson, reluctantly putting a normal amount of food on my plate since I wasn't too fond of egg noodles and beef stroganoff – at least not the way our dining hall cooked it. Jack seemed oblivious to the food's textures or lack of salt.. Jack supported Violet as she went on another rant about Kaito Cammish and what a sick monster he was.

"Do you know he messaged me about our Scottish place? The nerve of him. Isn't that right, Jack?"

"Yeah, babe. Totally. He's such a prick."

"He's just such a monster…"

She went on like that for a while. Jack never seemed to get bored of Vi's rants. He would ask her to explain every-thing two or three times with this look of fascination on his face.

I sat next to Crispin in our history class. I had two options, start praying my boredom away early or ask Crispin how he was holding up. A few minutes into our insanely boring lecture on Hadrian's wall, Crispin wrote on my note-book: I. AM. FREAKING. OUT.

Sigh. He could stand up to John Hewett and stab his roommate but reading his English essay out loud was driving him crazy. I could never understand this white boy...

I put my hand under the table and Crispin linked his fingers with mine. For a moment, I thought he might put my hand on his dick and try to get me to pull a Sarah Clifford. I mostly tried *not* to think about the fact that she'd *handled* my boyfriend, but it was impossible not to. Crispin didn't try anything, though. He just rubbed my hand and actually listened to the lecture.

I tried to take notes, but our presentation was so soon. That was way more important than dusty old Hadrian, whoever he was. All the Year 12s who planned our campaign sat together for dinner but by then, Crispin had gone nearly pale and was almost catatonic. Sarah Clifford eyed him with concern.

"Are we sure he's going to make it?"

I touched his back and Crispin didn't budge.

"He's fine. He's just processing. Getting ready," I answered hopefully. I didn't want him to lose his mind here, but he wasn't inspiring hope.

Vi stole a spear of asparagus off Jack's plate as he stole a bite of her steak.

"He'll be wonderful. Everyone loves Crispin," Vi said.

"Thanks," Crispin muttered.

He groaned and buried his head in his hands.

"Look at me. Paralyzed by public speaking. If my dad were here, he'd get the hot poker."

I wasn't sure if this was Crispin's idea of dark humor or if he was serious. Jack stepped in with some man-to-man advice.

"Go have a wank. It'll calm you down."

"Jack, that's disgusting!" Vi yelled.

I laughed and rubbed Crispin's back.

Then we argued about the wank for the next forty-five minutes and I think it actually helped Crispin forget how nervous he was. I held his hand for a while, but I don't know if that helped him as much as it helped me.

I had volunteered to be the first speaker for our campaign. If there was one thing John Hewett taught me, it was how to transform all those weird nervous jitters you get in front of other people into *charisma*. I didn't like getting myself into these situations, but I could whip out my charisma in a pinch.

My speech was about speaking out and how important it was to tell stories and trust people with what happened to us. I had come a long way from the traumatized girl who didn't trust anyone because I'd put my heart out there again and risked getting hurt. I worried that my speech was too heavy, but when I walked off stage, Crispin said it was perfect.

Vi, Sarah, Jack, and Mandy performed a skit after my speech. Mandy played the sexual predator for one bit and had to stop herself from giggling just like in rehearsals. She managed it okay and there was a standing ovation. Jack was the sexual predator in the next skit and he stumbled over a few of his lines but everyone clapped him through and the attention from the crowd helped him make it. Unlike Crispin, he thrived off attention like a golden retriever.

We did a few activities, breaking our small school up

into groups and after the hour or so of our planned activities, resources and recommendations for students and the administration, Crispin gave his speech. He was totally pale when he walked up on stage and he slouched his shoulders as much as he could. It would take more than some slouching to hide Crispin. He started nervously, stammering at first, but after a few minutes, the room was silent.

You could have heard a feather touch the ground. Crispin's voice always sounded nice, but he was musical when he explained things. He was serious and earnest too.

He cleared his throat before his finishing line.

"… we all have a duty to be better and to treat each other better. We are some of the most privileged people on the planet. What we do with that privilege defines us. Thank you for listening to our presentation, and I hope you can carry some of this with you into the future."

There was an explosion of applause. Crispin had done it! He was now turning really red and seemed to forget which way backstage was. He stumbled a bit, but then Jack led him off stage and Dean Leonard popped on to thank us for putting it all together. Vi and I hugged each other from excitement. Dean Leonard added a speech that was a touch self-congratulatory about Rapetti Academy providing the *perfect environment* for students to develop extra-curricular activities. *Yes, Agatha, we are incredible, but now we want to go home!*

Girls in LC stayed behind to help us tidy up. Crispin and Jack did the majority of the heavy lifting without complaint. I could feel my biceps getting shredded from all the stuff I was carrying. They ducked out of the auditorium for a few moments and then they both returned with *giant* bouquets of flowers for me, Vi, Mandy and Sarah Clifford.

"Surprise!" Jack announced. "We've helped but really this is all about the girls. Thanks for letting us tag along."

"Flowers!" Mandy said as Crispin handed her the enormous bouquet. "These are gorgeous. I *love* tulips."

"Thanks for helping me get out of my shell," Crispin said to her. Mandeep looked like she wanted to sink into the ground.

Crispin handed me my bouquet and kissed me. Hard.

"You are incredible," he murmured. "I would have totally fucked up if you didn't keep me on track all day. You are the best girlfriend. Ever."

Sarah turned red but she didn't say anything.

"You were great," I said to Crispin, trying not to rub it in Sarah's face.

"You were better. You got through all this talk and you just looked... mesmerizing."

"Thanks."

"Yeah, babe. Totally."

Jack handed Sarah her bouquet while Violet impatiently snatched hers.

"Jack, these are perfect!" She cooed. Sarah's cheeks turned red and she thanked the boys profusely too. We were about to leave and head our separate ways, when Jack Dyson pulled a gold key out of his pocket like the one Kaito handed Crispin.

"Has Cammish handed any of you one of these? It's been ages since I've attended a proper speakeasy party."

Crispin pulled his out of his pocket. Sarah Clifford pulled hers out of her pocket.

"Well," Sarah said. "We can all bring a plus one, so it looks like all of us are accounted for."

"Who are you going to bring?" Mandy asked.

"You, silly!" Sarah said. "I can't leave you out. Kaito's *such* a prick, but it'll be a great party."

Kaito Cammish throwing a great party? I had my doubts.

Chapter Twenty-One

We had a history test the night before Kaito's party and I totally messed it up. I wasn't amazing at history and English history brought out my inner desire to nap. How many men named Edward should be legally allowed to exist? Normally when I got bad grades, I tried to get extra credit, but Kaito's party was the night before Easter holiday, so I didn't have very much time to talk my way out of my C-. I just had to accept it. Sigh. At least I passed.

Crispin was sitting on my bed, eating some of Mandy's leftover curry while I searched through my clothes for something to wear. Mandy had just stepped out to help Julia get out of her corset. Julia snagged a golden key by offering to help Kaito with his Spanish homework. Mandy offered Crispin the leftover curry before hurrying off to help and he'd taken her up on the offer, munching down without a care in the world.

"I can't go to a stupid party when I have a C-!" I screamed at Crispin from beneath a pile of clothing I'd been digging through. He was too busy eating to care about the struggles of finding black clothes in a pile of black clothes.

"Sweetheart, you should have asked for help studying," Crispin said, wolfing down another giant bite.

"I don't need your stupid help," I snapped. "I need to find a way to *care* about British history."

"You can think of it as understanding my culture."

I grumbled under my breath after picking up the wrong pair of socks again, "I understand your culture. Drinking. Holidays. Passive Aggression."

"Right. Just like American culture is school shootings and electing racists," he said calmly.

I paused and stared at him with wide eyes.

"Damn, white boy. That was below the belt."

"Sorry…"

I rolled my eyes.

"Fine. Your culture is fish and chips, goofy sports and really tall, sexy, blond men."

"Don't forget curry," he said.

"Whatever."

"If you don't want to go to the party, I can pour the rest of this curry all over your breasts and lick it off. Who cares. Kaito will have my bollocks, but you'll be happy."

I wrinkled my nose.

"Please tell me that curry on my boobs is not a new kink."

Crispin shrugged and muttered, "I'd eat anything off you, babe."

"Hold on… did you just say that curry was British culture?!"

I was about to lecture Crispin about claiming curry of all

things as British culture, when Mandy hurried into the room carrying two dresses.

"Crispin, so sorry you have to hear this but Amina, do you really think I could pull off this pink?" Mandy gushed. "Julia thinks I should wear this one but I want to actually meet a boy tonight and have half a chance of getting laid. But I don't really do pink!"

"Why not? That dress is cute."

"What are you wearing?"

"Something black," I admitted.

"Oh my God, you're going to look amazing," she gushed at me. "Is the pink too much though? I don't want to look basic."

"No. It looks perfect," I assured her, picking up a black dress off my pile of black clothing. This one was cute but a little tight on me now. I held it up against my chest and Mandy nodded enthusiastically.

"Okay. You're right. I'll text Vi to double check," Mandy said, then she glanced at the dress I held over my body. "Ugh, I can't believe how beautiful you are, Amina. It's like… wow."

Crispin raised his fork and nodded sincerely.

"Mandy, we are in absolute agreement."

At least now I knew what I was going to wear. Mandeep Desai scurried off with her pink dress and I took my clothes off. Crispin set the curry down and watched me stumble out of my clothes, nearly tripping over my backpack. He chuckled at me as I caught my balance.

"Careful," he said.

"I'm *fine*," I grumbled, throwing the dress at Crispin while

I searched for a pair of tights and combat boots. March was a little warmer than February, but it was still blisteringly cold.

"I can't find any of my tights," I complained.

"Have you ever tried cleaning up?" Crispin asked, suddenly busying himself with the curry again.

"I don't have time to clean up!" I said again. "I can't find anything and I'm going to fail history because of some stupid *wanker* named Hadrian."

Crispin snorted.

"What did you just say?"

"Ugh, I'm even picking up your stupid lingo," I muttered.

"Your tights are over there," Crispin said, pointing to my lamp.

How did they get up there? I stretched as far as I could to reach them and slipped them on, turning around to look in my full-length mirror. I tried to push the hateful, critical thoughts out of my head. Frances Hewett didn't get to tell me how to live my life anymore. I couldn't help myself, though. I pinched my belly fat. Before I could pretend I totally wasn't doing that, I could see Crispin glaring at me in the mirror.

"If you're thinking something totally critical, stop," he said sternly.

"You can't control what I think, white boy," I snapped.

"I can control whether your bum gets a spanking..." Crispin muttered.

"Um... did you just threaten to beat me?" I folded my arms, giving Crispin a horrified look, but Crispin only grinned mischievously.

"There. Now you're not thinking all those awful things

when you look amazing. Now ditch the bra and shake for me…"

"I'm not doing a strip tease, white boy! Now where's my dress?"

Crispin shrugged and snatched the dress before I could get to it and he scrambled off the bed, holding it over his head. How had he gotten rid of the curry so quickly? He was *way* too fast. I jumped for the dress but Crispin caught me in mid-air and swung me over his shoulder.

"Crispin!"

"Gotcha…"

"Give me my dress!"

He set me on the bed and set the dress on my lap, giving me a firm kiss.

"Fine," he whispered. "I can't wait for the party. And I can't wait to take you to Barbados again."

"Promise me we won't run into your grandparents," I said as I shimmied away from Crispin and into the dress.

"I promise," He said. "But I'd promise you anything in that dress."

"It's not even on properly."

"And already, I want to rip it off."

I thought Crispin was about to make good on his promise to rip it off but when he touched my lower back, it was only to drag the zipper up my spine. I shivered and moved closer to his warmth as he zipped me up. He was so smooth and sensual.

"I love this," he whispered, kissing the back of my neck. "You look gorgeous."

Maybe, white boy. Maybe. I tried to wriggle away from

him to mess with my hair, but Crispin plopped me up on the bed and pressed his forehead to mine.

"Not so fast," he whispered.

"I wasn't going anywhere."

"I know," he whispered. "It's just… before we head out tonight, I need to tell you something."

Could we have *one* party at Rapetti that wasn't totally dramatic? My heart pulsed nervously and I only felt worse as Crispin's cheeks turned that telltale shade of pink.

"Spit it out."

"I can't get in touch with John anymore. I haven't heard from him in weeks and his girlfriend hasn't replied to my messages. He knows I'm coming to the island but… I don't know if… something's happened to him."

"You mean like murder?" I whispered.

I didn't know why anyone might want to murder John, but considering all the drama in the rest of Crispin's life and the situation with the 'little black book', I didn't know how much danger we could expect.

Crispin's brow pinched together and he nodded. I could tell it was painful for him. Too painful. Hearing that murder was something on the table made me worry a lot. I couldn't imagine how much it affected Crispin. I moved closer to him and this time, he let me.

"Yes," He muttered. "I don't want to believe it. I want to send Theo down there but he's… occupied."

I wanted to ask what Theo was occupied with — mostly to be nosy — but Crispin was really worried about John. I took his hand.

"He's probably doing a digital detox," I suggested about

Theo, who had the occasional hippie tendencies. "Don't worry. We'll be down there tomorrow night and we can figure everything out. We just need to get through this party and unwind."

"You're right," Crispin said. "It's just… If you didn't want to come anymore, I'd understand."

"I'm not letting you jump into danger on your own. Let's get Mandy and walk over to the house."

I didn't bother with makeup and I didn't fuss with my hair much. I was good to go. It was just Kaito Cammish's party.

"Walk?" Crispin said. "I'm not letting my *girlfriend* walk half a mile. Bring your friends. We'll take the car."

Chapter Twenty-Two

I don't know how we all piled in Crispin's car. Jack sat in the front with me and Violet on his lap (and Crispin threatening to maul him if he touched me under his breath). Mandy, Julia, Sarah Clifford, Trevor, Paige and Sarah G squeezed into the back seat.

"Does anyone have any cigarettes?" Paige asked.

"Here!"

Three hands shot out. Crispin cracked his bag window and ignored Trevor's shrieking as his turban flapped in the breeze, nearly yanking his head out the window.

"Watch it!' Sarah Clifford yelled as he dragged the turban back into the car and the flap smacked her in the face. Mandy screeched as Paige pretended to see a spider to scare her. Vi meanwhile worked diligently next to me opening a little baggie of pills and she popped one onto her tongue and one onto Jack's.

"These are for anxiety," she claimed. "Amazing effects, really."

I declined her mystery pill, but everyone in the back had

one. Jack stuffed one into his mouth "for later", even if Vi already gave him one, and he pulled out a tangerine from the same pocket.

"No!" Vi shrieked. "Not the bloody tangerine."

"Babe, I'm famished," Jack whined.

Before Vi could argue with him, Mandy reached out of the back and plucked the tangerine from his hand, throwing it out the window.

"Ha!" Vi said, ignoring Jack as he sank into a sulky silence.

"Anyone have any coke?" Julia asked, breaking up the awkward tension as Crispin swerved on the back roads to avoid hitting a house cat that had wandered into the middle of the street.

"Stubbins offered to sell me some. We're sorted," Paige said.

Our conversation was essentially that pointless until we got to the giant house. Kaito's "speakeasy party" was miles away from campus at a rented house, not the one close by — and it was the furthest all semester. Fifteen miles away was basically a long distance by English standards.

We'd worked out the 'secret location' as a team. Since our parties closer to campus roused suspicion, Kaito apparently found the funds for a luxurious rental. And by that I mean we all sent Crispin to shake him down and tell him to stop messing around if he wanted anyone to show up by selecting somewhere we could actually go safely.

The drive over there was down the most isolated and curvy country road I'd been on since arriving in England. The few cars we saw were all other Rapetti students and all luxurious vehicles like Crispin's. I sat in the front seat of

Crispin's car for our carpool over there. He didn't play any music, but he had the windows down as he drove at a reasonable speed for once down the isolated country road.

I stuck my hand out the window and tried not to let the wind mess my hair up too badly.

The rented castle for the party was deep into the countryside on a multi-acre estate with giant trees everywhere and pathways that wandered into dark forests. The whole place reminded me of Glottenham. Keys, plus ones, and party favors were completely managed for us. All we had to do was show up. But it felt like we were showing up somewhere dark and dangerous from the outside as Crispin slowed down to the parking lot.

As Crispin stared up at the turrets from the parking lot, I wondered if he was creeped out too or if it was just me. Violet, Jack and Paige were the others in the car, and we were all quiet as Crispin's car crunched along the gravel as he searched for a spot.

"It's bloody creepy," Paige said as Crispin parked and began the process of expelling us from his car. The castle looked like something out of a Dracula movie. If I really thought about it, Kaito was most likely in our year to be a vampire. Dark hair, a constant scowl on his face. Large, dark turrets and a thin but tall stone exterior gave the place a positively creepy air. The cold wind didn't hurt the overall creepiness. The night was almost as chilly as Halloween. Almost as chilly as the night I'd found August.

Crispin wrapped his arm around me as we all piled out of the car and stared at the castle. There were a few cars outside, but the doors almost looked sealed. The lawn was effortlessly silent. There had to have been at least thirty or forty people inside judging by the number of cars, but it was like the castle was soundproof.

"Do you think everyone's inside?" Vi whispered. "I'm getting so freaked out."

"It's the drugs babe," Jack whispered, running his hands over Vi's lips and making her giggle.

"Shut up," she whispered.

Jack grabbed her butt but this time, Vi didn't stop him.

"Let's go then," Crispin said with a grin. "Into Dracula's lair."

He linked arms with me and helped me navigate the rocks on the driveway. I didn't appreciate his terrifying comment. Boy, you know we're all afraid of Kaito!

"It's utterly silent out here," Mandy said awkwardly.

And then we were quiet until we got to the door.

Kaito himself thrust the door open like he had been watching us the entire time with a grin on his usually dour face. We could hear music pulsing loudly inside. The castle wasn't quiet... just soundproof. Even creepier. Crispin leaned over and whispered to me.

"Mr. Bainbridge owns this place and rents it out."

Vi was essentially walking into another castle *she* owned and she didn't even mention it to me. Damn, her dad must have had insane amounts of money.

Crispin continued softly, "He's close with Arthur Fox Senior. Benji's father. They were all close."

"Benji?" I giggled.

Crispin shrugged. "It's what we called him when we were kids."

I couldn't imagine the terrifying hairy half-Scotsman glowering through Glottenham being called something as cute as "Benji". Ugh, I just remembered I had to text Libby back. She always sent me sweet messages just trying to get me through the hard times at Rapetti Academy. Unfortunately, she couldn't send her former valedictorian status through the phone and my C- in history still loomed.

Crispin stuck his key out for Kaito's analysis.

"We demand entry into the speakeasy."

A handful of keys behind him flew into the air which Kaito appraised gleefully.

"Come on in, mate," Kaito said to Crispin, waving the rest of us inside. "And ditch the girl for a few minutes. We need to talk."

Crispin corrected him firmly and immediately, "She's not *the girl*."

"Right," Kaito said, sizing me up unimpressed as he dragged Crispin off. Mandy linked arms with me.

"Don't leave me," she whispered. "I don't really know anyone here."

She knew Julia and Paige, but maybe she didn't feel as close to them as she did to me, so I didn't mind her sticking close by.

Sarah Clifford got Mandy into the party, but she'd already ditched us to go hang out with Trevor and a few other girls from LR. Girls who didn't like me very much and girls who Mandy didn't know. My roommate was more shy than I'd realized.

"Okay," I said. "It's cool. We can get some drinks and then dance together. If you see a cute guy, I'll tell him to ask you to dance."

"That would be so embarrassing!" Mandy said.

"Mandy... have you ever dated anyone?"

She shook her head.

"No. I've tried hooking up but it's all gone... horribly wrong? The guys don't say yes. I just don't get it."

I gave Mandy a sympathetic look. It was a little cute to me how innocent she was about the world. And guys. I mean, she offered to give Crispin a blowjob which didn't seem innocent, but it was more misguided than anything else.

"Okay," I said, hoping to tease some information out of her. "Who do you have a crush on?"

"A *crush*?" She said horrified. "I don't have a crush. It's just... White guys don't like Indian girls. Guys at this school aren't exactly thrilled to bring Mandeep Desai home to Mummy. My parents basically expect me to marry a white boy because it's all I've known. It's just... their parents won't accept me, so they won't even look at me."

"Not everyone. Crispin's not like that."

"I am sorry to remind you of this, Amina, but his parents have unfortunately passed away. He can do whatever he wants now."

I folded my arms and eyed the room looking for a suitable crush for my roomie. I probed her more, "So you're saying you need a crush with dead parents?"

"Ugh, I'm a monster," Mandy moaned, burying her head in her hands.

"Don't worry girl," I said. "We can get you someone cute to dance up on."

Mandy looked at me like the idea of "dancing up on someone" was blasphemous.

"Like Devin?" She asked curiously.

I wanted to express my horror, but unfortunately, most people thought Devin was cute or at least "cute for a redhead" according to Sarah Clifford. Mandy obviously hadn't heard the thousands of rumors about Devin. Or the truth.

"Devin McLeod?" I repeated, as if maybe there was a secret superior Devin I might not have heard about yet. Since he'd been stabbed, I didn't think he would get out much partying. And if he did... would he come after Crispin for revenge? I was both nervous and concerned.

Mandy nodded.

"Girl, you don't want to go there."

"Why not?"

"I hooked up with him last year. Just no."

I didn't exactly want to advertise my chlamydia.

"Is that why Crispin stabbed him?" Mandy asked, her eyes widening at the prospect of romantic drama.

"I don't know. I hope not," I said, changing the subject back to Mandy's love life. "Trust me, Devin's an asshole."

"Does he have sex? I just want to have sex. I wouldn't even care if it was someone random or if he was bad. I'm tired of not losing its."

I bit down on my lower lip. Mandy didn't mean anything by that, but she didn't know what I would have given to be like her. A virgin, just worrying about finding someone nice and age appropriate. Not a creepy old man forcing me. Not John Hewett's house of horrors.

I tried to *be* normal for her.

"Okay... so you like Devin... Who else is on the football team?"

Only the hottest for my roommate!

We ruled out Felix Stubbins and Jack Dyson for different, but obvious reasons. Noah wouldn't date anyone who wasn't Jewish. By the time we'd made it through the whole team,

Mandy was just getting dejected. A hand reached over her shoulder. She turned around stunned to see who it was. Kaito Cammish.

I glared at him and got ready to kick him in the nuts if necessary. He stuck out a hand to Mandy. He wore a gold ring with an enormous ruby in it on his index finger and he had a tattoo saying "GET FUCKED" on the saddle of his thumb.

"Mandeep," Kaito asked politely. "Would you like to dance?"

Chapter Twenty-Three

Mandy gazed up at Kaito as if she couldn't believe he was talking to her. She took his hand and I looked at her like she had two heads. Kaito's hands slipped around her waist effortlessly. I wanted to rip him off her, but Mandy waved me away. Kaito smiled and it was seriously the most unnatural thing I'd ever seen. I was about to stage a rescue when Crispin's hand clasped around mine.

"Hello, Twiggy. Enjoying the party?" Crispin asked, a grin lighting up his face once he saw me. I had bigger concerns than flirting with Crispin. I gestured as subtly as I could to Kaito and Mandy.

"Do you see what's happening?" I hissed.

"Two consenting adults dancing. Like we ought to be. It's our last big night before Easter break, Twiggy. I want it to be perfect."

"Perfect? Have we ever had a *perfect* party here? I'd take normal."

Crispin pulled on a coil of my hair gently, then pushed it out of my face before giving me a kiss on the cheek.

"We're in a demented castle with electronic music pulsing everywhere. We could explore. We could find a dark hallway to make out in. We could kick some art freaks out of an upstairs bedroom and… you know… shag."

"Is that seriously all you're thinking about?"

I raised my eyebrow suspiciously, even if I wasn't opposed to "shagging" as Crispin put it. He grinned and took in my outfit one more time.

"I'm totally fucked up about Barbados," he said, nervously fluffing out his hair. "But I want to be with you. I want to forget it all."

"Then let's do it white boy. Let's party."

Crispin reached into his pockets for something, shuffling about with his giant hands.

"Kaito sold me this," he said.

Then Crispin pulled out two of the biggest joints I'd ever seen.

"We can't finish those on our own."

Crispin grinned. "Jack and Vi can join us," he suggested.

I nodded and gave him two thumbs up, wrapping my arms around my giant white boy, swaying to the music. Crispin grabbed my waist and held his wrapped joints next to my head. They didn't smell as good as the stuff in Theo's stash but it smelled like strawberry cheesecake and gasoline.

I moved my hips to the music as he touched me and Crispin's hands found my hip bones. He ran his thumbs over the protruding bones, which were slightly less skeletal than in the fall. Healing. I'd been healing. And now, we were both doing more than healing. Our bodies pressed together and I clung to Crispin more tightly.

"Dancing," Crispin murmured. "I can do dancing."

"Are you sure, white boy?"

"I dunno. I like when you do that belly dancing stuff."

"Belly dancing?"

"I dunno. With your hips," he whispered. "You're *really* good at it."

I laughed and Crispin lowered his head shyly, blond hair cascading over his face. I pushed some of Crispin's hair out of his face and then tiptoed up to kiss him, moving my hips against him. Whatever 'belly dancing' Crispin was talking about, I appeared to be doing properly because he grabbed my hips and kissed me hard.

Tomorrow morning, we'd head down to Barbados for exactly three days to find John Braithwaite and ask him questions. Crispin was insistent that we not spend too much time down there for both of our safety.

There had been signs we should lay low. My mom had sent me 4 emails trying to convince me to visit her as she "coped with the divorce", but I did my best to ignore her. Daddy had also wired more money into my account, but it wasn't enough to get me to talk to him again.

He hadn't tried to talk to me recently. The money was just a reminder. *I'm still watching.* Hopefully, he wasn't looking too hard.

I tried to hold out hope that our simple mission to Barbados would be a success, and I knew Crispin was still worried about John but for now, kissing me appeared to be a great distraction for both of us. We were kissing so hard on the dance floor that I stopped hearing the music and I could only feel my hot boyfriend's body beneath my fingertips. I wanted more. I wanted to take Crispin upstairs and... well, you know the rest.

When I pulled away from him for a moment, I could see Mandy and Kaito grinding against each other in an extremely awkward manner. Kaito bent his knees a lot to match Mandy's petite height and he swayed more like a pendulum than anything else. There were other couples in the crowd and a few groups of female friends dancing together. Three boys on the rugby team who were too cool to care leaned against the wall watching the dancers.

Crispin glanced over his shoulder, his lips narrowing into a thin line as he glanced at Mandy and Kaito, who were dancing like nobody was watching.

"They seem to be hitting it off."

I rolled my eyes.

"It's Kaito. Tell him to leave my roommate alone. He's not good enough for my home girl."

I danced around Crispin, who watched me as I put my moves on him.

"It looks like Mandy's handling him fine," he said half-heartedly as he stared at my butt.

It looked like Mandy was putting her number in his phone. *Girl, no!* He had been responsible for the night with me, Violet, Crispin and the knives. Except Kaito had done much worse and showed no remorse.

Before I could run over there and save her, Crispin snuck his hand into mine and pulled me away. He texted Jack with his other hand as we took one of the back staircases to the bedrooms upstairs. The first thing we smelled was vinegar and tobacco from the top floor. There were sex noises coming out of half the rooms.

Crispin grinned as he glanced down the hallway.

"Russian roulette. Which door should we choose?"

"That one."

We picked a room and thankfully, the door opened and there wasn't anyone having sex in the bed. Or on the floor. And hopefully not in the closet either. Crispin checked. He pulled the rug out from its spot beneath the bed into the center of the floor, and sat on it, pulling a lighter out of his breast pocket.

"They're on their way. Here. You start it."

He stuck the joint in my mouth and I made a cup around it so Crispin could light me up. Phew. That first hit nearly knocked me out. Crispin patted my back gently as I coughed.

"There, there."

"Where did Kaito get this stuff?"

"I dunno. Probably Amsterdam."

I passed the joint to Crispin and he took in a huge hit, his giant chest puffing up before he exhaled.

"Fuck. This is good, babe. Come closer."

I moved closer to Crispin and he put his arm around me before passing me the joint again. Jack and Vi came into the room, giggling and tipping drinks into each other's mouths. Vi plopped next to me and Jack sat down, reaching for a tangerine in his pocket after leaning over to kiss Vi on the lips.

"Vi, babe. I love you."

"Jack, stop."

"I really love you. I'd die for you. Seriously. I'd give up my last tangerine ever for you."

Crispin passed Vi the joint and she took three massive puffs in a row.

"Wow. Crispin…" she said, squeezing her chest with her hand to stop herself from coughing. "This is incredible."

"We have Kaito to thank."

Vi scowled, passing the joint to Dyson.

"Kaito… he's such an an arsehole."

"I don't think we can say that about the Japanese anymore," Jack said seriously.

"What does this have to do with him being Japanese?" Vi protested.

"I dunno. But we can't bully them anymore. I learned that in secondary. Huge incident."

"That's horrific," Vi said.

"I only took on people smaller than me," Jack said. "It's instinct, you know. The bigger eat the weak."

There was no way Violet could get into this conversation without it turning into an argument. Crispin curled his knees up and took the joint from Jack Dyson, pressing his finger to his lips in hopes that his idiotic friend wouldn't get Vi started on another hour long rant.

"What are you two doing tomorrow?" Vi asked, ignoring Jack's comments.

I glanced at Crispin nervously. I didn't know how secret our plans were meant to be.

"Barbados," he said.

"Lucky!" Vi said.

Jack grinned. "I'm dragging her to Mum's apartment complex in Hong Kong. We're going to eat fried shrimp, bathe in hot tubs and have lots of sky rise sex."

"Jack! We *won't* be having sex if you keep telling people about it."

"What's wrong with telling people. I'm proud of you, babe. You're like... spicy."

"Spicy? You don't *like* spicy anything. You won't even have curry."

"Yeah, but... I like you."

Crispin laughed. I took another hit of the joint but I was too high to laugh. All I wanted to do was snuggle up next to Crispin and float away. A normal Rapetti party. Maybe it was possible after all. We smoked and hung out together for a while. Then we went back downstairs to dance. Kaito's party was shockingly good. No fights. No cheating. There was plenty of food and alcohol.

Kaito and Mandy had left the dance floor and sat at the foot of the stairs talking to each other like old friends.

I wanted to rescue her but she looked... happy. I made a mental note to at least give her a fair warning later. Mandy had been a good friend so far, she'd probably do the same for me. Jack and Vi left the party early. Crispin hung out with the football boys for a bit and I danced with some of the other LC girls who Kaito had invited. Crispin found me again and this time, he really wanted to leave. When he wrapped me in a big warm hug, I felt why growing between his legs. I raised an eyebrow and glanced up at him suspiciously.

"Really?"

"Tomorrow, we have to fly *commercial*. I'll be recognized," he said. We had to fly commercial to stay "low key" and his grandparents wouldn't expect our arrival.

"That doesn't explain why your dick is pressing into me."

"Anxiety horniness?" Crispin murmured, making his best effort to nibble at me.

Boys. They think everything is about their dicks.

"I'm losing you, aren't I? I'd better carry you off before you change your mind."

"I can walk to the car on my own, white boy."

"Want to race me?"

"No."

Crispin ran. So I raced him. And even if he was really fast, he also had a lot to smoke and drink. For once, I got to the car first and I properly beat him. He stared at me bewildered.

"I can't believe you beat me."

"Are you that surprised?"

"You were *fast*."

"Uh huh."

"Have you ever considered running?"

"Sports?"

"Yes," Crispin gasped, grabbing his chest. "I was actually trying."

"I'm full of surprises, white boy," I said, even if I didn't really have any surprises and this was just a weird fluke.

Crispin shook his head.

"Get in the car," he said. "I've got to call Freddie before the night's out. I'll need her back at the cottage with Katrina by the time we're done in Barbados."

"You know where she is?"

"Scotland," Crispin said bluntly. "But I want her back in England for the summer. It's coming at us fast. The anniversary of their deaths. It's the first year since they've been gone and somehow, I feel worse than the morning I discovered them except for you, Amina."

I leaned over and then Crispin kissed me. His fingers tangled in my hair as we kissed. We both knew we wouldn't be leaving his car until we'd made love several times. I crawled over the seats onto Crispin's lap, the growing tent in his pants only serving to arouse me more. Crispin's hips rushed to my waist and then the second part of our night began...

He didn't even care if anyone saw. Or maybe he liked it. I kissed him back hard, losing my ability to care too. I was just happy that we were together.

Chapter Twenty-Four

"I can't believe people stand in lines," Crispin grumbled after we checked in and bustled through security. "I thought first class meant you got... I dunno... a golf cart or something."

"You are so spoiled."

"Spoiled? This is *oppression*. If I were the Prime Minister, everyone would get a private jet."

"Crispin, have you ever heard of emissions?"

"They'd be solar-powered."

Boy, bye!

My credit card gave us access to these fancy private lounges that Daddy liked waiting in between flights. I never used them on my own because I didn't travel much and when I did, old weird business men would hit on me so I preferred sitting with the normal people. No one would dare hit on me with Crispin standing next to me.

I checked us in and a kind woman brought us a cup of coffee.

"Thank you," Crispin said to her. "Unfortunately, this doesn't look nearly strong enough to qualify as coffee."

He refused to take the cup.

"I'll take both," I said, snatching both cups and then glaring at Crispin.

"Are you crazy?"

"No. Not entirely."

"She was being nice."

"This entire experience is unsettling. I had to take my shoes off in public. I had to see a man's arse crack as he removed his belt. This is *barbaric*."

I rolled my eyes. Crispin was giving drama queen. I didn't realize he found such normal things confusing. I wanted to make his transition into real life easy, but Crispin couldn't have been crankier about the entire situation.

"Barbaric? It's called being normal," I explained calmly. He slouched into his shoulders, desperate to be invisible.

"Normal? No wonder everyone *normal* is so bloody miserable," Crispin grumbled. I could tell I was going to have to smack the man-child out of him or find another way to cope with his miserable personality until we got there.

"You're drinking the shitty coffee," I told him firmly, shoving it into Crispin's hands. "You need caffeine so you can stop being such a grouch."

He rolled his eyes and took a sip, contorting his face in horror.

"You can't expect me to consume this inferior rubbish," he said so snobbily that his accent literally changed.

I glared at him for the affected posh accent and his rude ass commentary before responding, "Um, yes I can. You aren't going to embarrass me in public, white boy."

The private lounge wasn't exactly "public", but compared to a private jet, it felt like being an animal at the zoo. Crispin sneered at our surroundings – which a normal person would have considered a luxurious reprieve from sitting on the airport floor or those uncomfortable hard seats in every airport in the United Kingdom.

"Public. Thank goodness we aren't in public. Did you notice those people gawking at me?" Crispin said, huffing in offense. They were probably looking at him because he was a giant.

I'd pretended not to notice, but Crispin hadn't been wrong in his estimation that people stared at him everywhere he went. That only stopped when we stepped into the British Airways private lounge.

"I'd fly Virgin, but the Bransons are all cunts," Crispin muttered.

He'd called seventeen people cunts since we got here under his breath. He *really* didn't like attention. *Boy, you can't keep this sexy from the world forever!* I rolled my eyes again.

"Just relax. We'll be in Barbados soon and when we aren't fighting crime, we can have sex in the ocean with sea turtles swimming around us…"

"I'm *not* taking my cock out around a sea creature's mouth."

"Ew! Who said anything about its mouth."

"Well it might mistake me for food. I wouldn't chance it," Crispin said smirking, his mood improving slightly.

Crispin took another anguished sip of the coffee and then made another face.

"Fuck's sake, Amina. I can't drink this."

"Add milk and sugar," I snapped. "And deal."

"Since when did you get so dominant," Crispin muttered.

"Excuse me?" I said as sassily as I could muster, letting Crispin know I would bring trouble if he didn't chill out a bit.

"Nothing."

I rolled my eyes. Crispin needed to stop stressing out about everything.

"Have you heard from John?" I asked him, hoping that he'd have some good news for a change. Crispin shook his head.

"Like I said, John is probably deep into his island-themed digital detox," I said hopefully, even if I had no proof that anything of the sort was happening.

"I think I can find where his girlfriend lives," Crispin said.

"How?" I asked.

Crispin shrugged, momentarily distracted from his complaints by his drive to solve the mystery of John's whereabouts.

"Small island. I know her family name. I ought to be able to track her down."

I had my doubts that this would be as easy as Crispin thought, but I was still willing to help him out.

"So our plan is to go down there and stalk your uncle's ex-girlfriend."

"Right. Then accuse my uncle of being there the night my parents died, even if it's utterly ridiculous since he lives in the Caribbean."

I didn't point out to Crispin that he thought it was utterly ridiculous that John might have been related to him in the first place. He couldn't exactly trust his instincts when it came to utterly ridiculous.

"You know what?" Crispin said softly, leaning over and kissing my cheek.

"What?"

"With Novak out of the picture, I'm second in the class," he said, suddenly changing the subject to grades. My grades were terrible and I didn't want to talk about them, but Crispin enjoyed reveling in any form of domination over his enemies.

"Are you serious?" I said, squirming in embarrassment at the thought of what my grades could be.

"I study loads," Crispin protested. "And I'm modestly intelligent. I've got a legacy to uphold. I can't show up at Rapetti and *fail*. It would be unacceptable."

Boy, bye! How the heck did Crispin care so much about his grades. I just didn't get it.

"What about having fun and just hanging out?" I asked, more interested in my next nap than my next midterm.

"College isn't about having fun. It's about preparing for university," Crispin said, as if this was a widely held belief.

I wrinkled my nose. "Why do you need university? You don't need a job. You're basically like a millionaire. I'm the one who needs to find a job and get my act together."

Crispin's cheeks turned red. I was lowkey jealous of his good grades and acting like a hater, but he was the one acting like he was under the microscope.

"Stop," he whispered. "Don't say that. It's... rude."

"That's rude?" I said, rolling my eyes. "Boy, bye."

Crispin drank some more of the coffee and made another face. I get it, Crispin, super rich people have better coffee. The private lounge attendant turned on the television.

Crispin grew visibly angry and muttered under his breath, "Fuck's sake. Can you go *anywhere* without watching the bloody news."

I gazed up at the bright screen instinctively. The TV was silent with half-useful closed captions running along the bottom. I half expected to see a report about Crispin's parents again. That was usually why he avoided the television. Unfortunately, I saw something that made me understand Crispin better than I'd ever wanted to.

The closed captions seemed to slow down.

Presidential hopeful Texas Republican John Hewett holds his first rally today in Dallas. Over 300,000 people attended the rally, many of them sporting signs supporting conspiracy theories that Rush Limbaugh is really Jim Morrison. Ted, what do you think of that?

I didn't give a damn what Ted thought about my father's speech. I didn't give a damn about my father's speech. I zoned out through Ted's thoughts and tried to look away from the screen. If Crispin was trying not to look, he was failing just as badly as I was. I read the closed captions of my father's speech, and I felt sick to my stomach. I wanted to shut it off but... I couldn't stop myself from watching and reading...

The problem with America today is, we're too divided. Daughters want nothing to do with their fathers. Sons want nothing to do with their mothers. No one has a clue about family values in this country. No one has a clue about Christian values in this country. In Texas, we believe the Bible comes before everything else. And the Bible punishes loose women. It doesn't reward them with food stamps.

I thought I was going to be sick. I could tell that Daddy was putting a lot of effort into this and there were probably

$300,000 Hewett-American dollars that went into picking out his stupid tie for the rally.

Even with the TV moving silently, I could hear Daddy's voice like it was in my head. I suddenly felt like a thousand pairs of eyes fixed on me, even if Crispin and the attendant were the only people there. No one else had arrived to wait for their flight yet, or they were all content with the public waiting area.

Crispin leaned over and put his arm around me, holding me close.

"Close your eyes," he whispered. "Pretend it isn't happening. Just for now. I promise you, Twiggy, I haven't forgot my pledge to protect you. That man will never have absolute power. Not as long as I am alive."

I wanted to believe his promise more than anything, but I already knew the truth. Nothing could stop John Hewett from having absolute power over me. Crispin was like a tiny sandbar against a tidal wave of hate and power. He was from one of the richest and oldest American political dynasties. Crispin might be rich, but the English had their money tied up in estates and investments.

The Hewett's played monopoly with their money.

I was just lucky Daddy had taken his eye off me for a while. He had bigger fish to fry. Mom was on her divorced vibe — she'd even posted a bikini picture to her private social media account, which had prompted comments from all her former sorority sisters about her "new era".

Ella Novak was on the loose, probably gone for now. I wanted to hold out hope about that, but I supposed you could never be sure.

Thinking about daddy filled me with deep anxiety and dread unlike anything I had ever felt. It was as if someone had ground their fingers into my internal organs and massaged them painfully around my abdomen. The grip he had on me was tight, even when he was thousands of miles away. What would happen if he won an election? What would happen if the public never knew the truth?

I had finally told the truth about him to my friends at school. Some people guessed my speech at the sexual assault awareness campaign was about him. But this news felt like a setback to my progress – and a punch to the ribs that knocked the wind out of me effortlessly.

My abusive adoptive father, John Hewett, was running for president of the United States. The horrible, violent, criminal who had abused me, hurt my boyfriend and preyed on everyone he set his hands on could become the most powerful man in the United States.

How long could I avoid a man with infinite power? How far was it even possible for me to run?

I didn't want Crispin to hurt him. Not because I cared about him getting hurt, but because I didn't want Crispin to go to jail. He had already come so dangerously close to that. I couldn't bear it. I couldn't bear losing my boyfriend. I'd tried a breakup but the thought of letting Crispin go was impossible.

I just... wanted him.

My hands locked with Crispin's and not a single part of me wanted to let go. We'd figure this out together: his parents' murder, freeing me from John Hewett *and* university. Maybe Crispin could get me to care about that.

My phone buzzed and I realized our flight was boarding. *Time for us to handle our shit, white boy. You and me against the world.* I held Crispin's hand and prepared myself mentally for the firestorm ahead. Our fingers interlaced and I felt right then that I would never let that man go. *Never.*

Chapter Twenty-Five

We never found John. I didn't think our trip was useless, but we definitely didn't meet our objective. Everything about being in Barbados felt strange and unfamiliar, like we didn't belong.

John's "girlfriend" was no longer seeing him and her bubbly personality had changed since I last met her. She emphasized that John was her *ex*-boyfriend and barely wanted to speak to Crispin. Her mother and sister stood by her side in the doorway of the house where Crispin tracked her down, so there wasn't much he could do about her not wanting to talk to him.

But it was more than that. I could tell she was scared, and she wanted nothing to do with the Barclay family. Giving me a sympathetic look, she suggested that we both ought to go back to England. Her family seemed kind enough.

She invited us to a big family meal, but she was clear. We were in over our heads and John scared her. She mentioned that he'd ramble on about his plans and needing to go to London, but she was certain that he hadn't left the island because she knew people who worked at the airport. Crispin couldn't convince her to give any reasons for her sudden fear of John, or distance from the family.

So we learned nothing in Barbados. No details about John, no details about the hard drive and we barely avoided Crispin's grandparents. On the bright side, we spent lots of time on the boat, smoked lots of Theo's good weed and had lots of crazy sex.

Crispin's little studio apartment at the golf club had been both quaint and cozy, but after we failed to find John, his mood soured considerably. I tried to cheer him up by talking about Vi and Jack's photos from Hong Kong or Mandeep's weekend trip to Rotterdam with Misaki and Julia Anders. He didn't even cheer up when Freddie called him to complain about Katrina and announce her plans to return to the cottage in the summer.

He just asked where both of them were and hung up in a fury when Freddie made an excuse about staying away from him *until* summer to look after her mental health. I knew the one year anniversary of his parents death was approaching. It was everywhere on TV in Barbados — at least all the venues that catered to English people. I avoided American news, but I knew they were reporting on my dad's presidential campaign incessantly. He was popular, and that scared the crap out of me. What if he won? Crispin hardly wanted to leave the apartment or the boat. At least all the time on the boat I got to look at him shirtless and we had plenty of sex.

On the flight back to England, Crispin was detached and solemn, only leaning over to kiss me when I'd pinch his thighs for attention. Three nights in Barbados and we'd already have to brave the time change again. Ugh. I would be a sleepy mess once we returned to London and our trip disappointed Crispin even if I'd been happy to catch some sun and see some people who looked like me. I loved Barbados.

Despite that, I couldn't wait to see Libby. She'd been messaging me and keeping me up with her pregnancy. Now she would have a pair of twin boys and a pair of twin girls. I loved Libby's pictures of Sophie and Kiojah, the twin girls, and I couldn't wait to see what other cute genetic combinations she and Benjamin Fox would produce. Libby was a few weeks away from her due date and Ben invited us to spend the rest of our spring break with their family in London. Benjamin and Libby stayed in a big townhouse in London with plenty of spare bedrooms.

The freckles on Crispin's nose spread out and covered up the makings of a serious burn. His face was reddened and tight with frustration when we arrived in London, and not just because we had to fly commercial again. Getting Crispin all the amenities and upgrades of first class did nothing to improve his mood.

When we arrived in London, Ben's driver met us at the airport and drove us to their townhouse. Crispin calmed down once we were away from the majority of the public and tucked away in the back of a private car. He grew more affectionate, sliding his arms around me and keeping his body close to mine.

Ben and Libby weren't in at the precise moment we arrived, which was standard for them since they traveled very often, but the nannies were there with their daughters as the housekeeper led me and Crispin to our guest bedroom. There was a little card on the nightstand.

This is usually Theo's room but we moved him over so you could hang! See you later tonight. — Libby & Ben

Crispin flopped back on the bed and groaned, "I flew commercial for nothing."

"Not nothing," I whispered, crawling on top of Crispin and resting my head on his chest. "We played in the sun. We had three days of fun."

Crispin touched my back and held me against him. His body felt so excessively large beneath mine. I liked it. He was firm, muscular and safe – everything I wanted and needed. Sometimes, I couldn't figure out which of my personality traits had won Crispin over. From my perspective, I offered him very little.

I couldn't protect him. I couldn't keep him safe. Love was all messed up in my head because of what I'd been through. But he still held me close, like I was precious, and I loved him just for that. Crispin sighed as he adjusted his grasp around me.

"You're right, Lips. It's just... this won't go away on its own, I don't think. Someone has that hard drive and I don't know what they intend to do with it or what's really on it."

"How long has it been since you've heard from Freddie?"

"Three days. Freddie's off her rocker again. Katrina's driving her mad. I want them to come back but Freddie says she prefers Scotland. I don't even know how they found accommodations, since they're both utterly useless. I don't bother asking. The bills come and I pay them just the way Dad did."

I scrunched my lips up and kissed Crispin's neck. He chuckled and pulled me tighter against his chest.

"Oh, Lips. Listen to me. A beautiful woman on my chest

and I can only moan... want to bet Ben and Libby have an incredibly well-stocked fridge? I'm *starving*."

Before I could point out that Crispin was always starving, he hoisted me over his shoulder and carried me out of the guest room. He at least allowed me to walk to the kitchen with some dignity, although I had to run back to the room to throw on another giant sweater. Crispin spoke to the chef in whispered French and then sat next to me as she cooked. He rubbed his hand on my thigh and sighed.

"This summer, Lips... I don't want you mixed up in all this."

"What does that mean?"

"The Freddie stuff. My dead parents. I want you to go to America and... I'll stay here and sort my life out."

"Like... we break up?"

"No. Long distance. For a few weeks."

"Great. So I'll be all alone and vulnerable to attack from every direction while you're having the time of your life and possibly falling in love with a stripper."

"Where would I meet a stripper?" Crispin said, looking very upset with me for even saying something like that. I couldn't help my insecurity. After everything we'd been through, it didn't make sense to me that Crispin would suddenly want to be apart.

It didn't take too long for me to become conscious of my panic.

"It could happen," I said defensively. "And the attack could definitely happen."

Crispin's lips pursed. I knew he wouldn't let anything happen to me, even if he left, but I didn't like the idea of being alone.

"So you're not loving the idea," Crispin responded astutely. How could he expect me to be in the same country as my father? Sure, America was huge, and you could fit the entire United Kingdom several times over in all the land between Texas and a place on the East Coast, like New York, but I still didn't feel safe there.

"No. I'm not. I don't want to go to America," I said firmly, in disbelief that Crispin would suggest such a thing.

"What about your parents?" Crispin asked. Was he out of his mind?

I didn't hesitate before responding to him rudely, "John and Frances can kiss my black ass."

Crispin's nose turned red and the chef pretended like she wasn't holding back laughter. I meant what I said. John's stupid presidential speeches were still clogging the airwaves. Frances was *still* in England which probably meant she hadn't done anything to confront my adoptive father about what he did to me. She was in her "divorce era", which apparently didn't include atoning for anything she'd done to me.

"Okay," Crispin said, leaning over and kissing my shoulder. "I meant your birth parents."

"Right, the people who sold me down the river. I don't care about them either."

"You don't know the entire story," Crispin said.

"Crispin, I get you have 'dodgy past' but defending the people who sold their kid is not the way forward."

"I'm not defending them. It's just... John Hewett's a scumbag. Isn't there a chance they aren't terrible people and he's lied?" Crispin said. My ears were instantly hot. I knew Crispin wanted the best for me, but this level of optimism was delusional.

"I'm not that lucky," I grumbled.

I thought Crispin would pounce on me for saying that but he just sighed.

"I know the feeling, babe," he said, hugging me closer and planting a kiss on my head. The kiss made me feel a little better, but Crispin had said words he couldn't take back and activated thoughts about my birth parents that I hadn't been eager to acknowledge.

"Thank you."

Crispin twirled some of my hair around his fingers and he whispered, "I still think you ought to try. You owe it to that little girl."

"What little girl?"

"The little girl after the storm searching for someone to hold onto," he said.

I fell into an uncomfortable and contemplative silence, which didn't appear to bother Crispin, mostly because the chef served us up shortly after. It wasn't completely crazy to assume that John Hewett would lie. But what about the documents? What about Frances?

The worst part was not even knowing what I wanted. Would learned more about my birth parents actually help my situation, or just make me feel worse? What if they were terrible?

I couldn't think about food until Crispin made me. It took him a while to notice that I was just watching him eat. He was normally pretty perceptive about my food intake, but starvation slowed him down for a while. He hunched over and ate like a starved wolf until he'd finished half his food.

"Eat," Crispin commanded. I picked at the green beans

and steak for a few minutes before Crispin glared and I picked up the pace of my eating.

His greed overwhelmed his noble mission because once Crispin finished consuming his lunch, he picked around the edges of my plate, apologizing in a huff when I pricked his palm with the sharp ends of my fork.

He stuck some of my hair behind my ear and then sighed.

"I suppose I've made you terribly upset with the long distance thing," he said. "It's not that I want to be without you. It's just... I wonder if you'll forgive me if I take this chance away from you."

I assumed he meant the chance to find out more about my past. I hadn't mentioned anything about it recently, so it honestly felt like just an excuse. Crispin bringing it up again made me scowl.

I poked at my plate bitterly and said, "If you want to dump me, man up and dump me."

"Dump you?" Crispin said. "Why the bloody hell would I want that? Don't be ridiculous. I'm keeping you, Amina. And I don't care who likes it."

"What if I don't like it?"

Crispin ignored me and continued telling me his plan, which he'd put more thought into than I realized. "I've been researching houses in New Orleans."

"Crispin!"

"I'm serious," he said pleadingly. "I've got stuff going on and before it all happens... I want to make sure I've looked after you."

"Okay. Sounds... sketchy."

"Sketchy?"

"You know... weird."

"Right," Crispin muttered. "Anyway. It's 6 million dollars in the 14th ward. Columns. Chandeliers. Incredible closet space. I really think you'd like it. There's even a pool."

"You're buying a house?"

Crispin shrugged and muttered, "It's not my first. I'm 18 after all."

"You can't just *buy* a summer house."

"Too late."

"You bought it?"

"The title's in your name. It'll be leased for the next year and if you like it, it's yours forever. If you don't, I'll burn it. Surprise."

"What's this for?"

"For the summer."

I raised a suspicious eyebrow and teased Crispin a bit, "No... what is it *for*? Did I do like a good sex thing? Was it my dancing?"

I wriggled my hips suggestively.

"I love you," Crispin said both simply and urgently. "I don't need a reason. It's just money, Amina. If you want, I'll come visit on the weekends for a few hours. What's a bit of jet lag to make you happy."

"I'm not doing this long distance thing. Thanks for the house, but you're coming with me."

"Sweetheart, I've also bought you a car. I don't like American cars, so it's a brand new white Jaguar."

The way Crispin pronounced *jaguar* should have been illegal but the sound of a new car made it incredibly sexy at the moment.

"Are you serious?"

"Yes, I'm serious. It's called planning. I want you to have an amazing summer with or without me."

"With you," I snapped. "Because we're spending the summer together."

Before I could attack Crispin even more for his dumb "long distance" idea that involved having sex like zero times for my entire hot girl summer, the doors to Han's Place — yes, Ben and Libby's London house had a name — swung open. Benjamin and a *very* pregnant Libby walked in together.

"Crispin Barclay!" Ben called loudly. "I can smell you from the entryway."

Libby pinched Ben.

"He's joking!" She said, groaning. "But my back *really* hurts, so I won't be able to hang out long."

We rushed to greet them excitedly. Ben and Libby were a whole vibe! I loved Libby's energy and now that she was extremely pregnant, she looked like a goddess. Damn, girl. Goals! Not like I wanted to give my white boy any ideas about knocking me up. I had other goals too! I just hadn't figured them out yet.

We helped Ben and Libby to their parlor and I finally got to meet their daughters. OMG. Cutest kids ever.

"They look just like you," I told Libby. Ben shifted uncomfortably and I got the sudden sense I'd said the wrong thing.

"They're actually my half-sisters," Libby said. "I adopted them after my mom died."

"Oh. I'm so...I'm so sorry."

"Don't be," Benjamin said, putting a protective hand on Libby's shoulder. "They were a gift, just like Libby. They're *our* daughters."

Wow. I guess some people who adopted others were

normal. Just not my parents. The thought made me suddenly sad.

The conversation moved to Barbados and our failure of a trip. Ben listened eagerly to Crispin detailing everything. Crispin kept Sophie on his lap and Libby kept Kiojah on hers. The twins had *such cool names*. Libby explained that they knew Crispin well from the summer.

Crispin looked hot holding a baby. I just got the feeling that Crispin would be a good dad. That couldn't happen for us anytime soon. I ignored the weird pang of desire.

"Any plans for the summer then?" Ben asked, rolling up the sleeves on his white button down shirt. "Will you pursue researching Amina's parents?"

Chapter Twenty-Six

"Certainly," Crispin said, as if it were his decision to research my parents. Ben glanced at Crispin and then toward me.

"I don't know if there's a point," I said.

"There's a point," Libby said. "Knowing the truth."

"What if the truth sucks?" I asked, which I thought was a fair question. Both Ben and Crispin weren't sure what to say.

Libby tried to reassure me.

We spent the rest of the evening with our friends and their daughters. Kiojah and Sophie were the only babies I knew, but they were officially my favorite babies. I played with Kiojah's hair and then peekaboo with Sophie, who had an infectious laugh. They were *so stinking cute*. Ben seemed to really love them and love being a dad. I'd never seen him in dad mode yet, but he was sweet.

Ben told us detailed stories about both of his daughters and his eyes gleamed when he spoke. The scowl that appeared to be a permanent fixture on his face turned out not to be so permanent once he talked about Sophie and Kiojah.

I tried my best to forget that we'd had such an unsuccessful trip to Barbados during out hangout. After, in bed, Crispin snuggled me closely and tried to fall asleep but he never slept much when he worried, especially about his parents. I couldn't sleep because Ben and Libby were making me think about mine. Crispin kept gushing about his 6 million dollar find in New Orleans and I couldn't imagine what I'd do there alone, or how I'd approach introducing myself to my birth parents. What if I had the wrong couple?

At around 2 in the morning, we were both definitively awake. No chance of falling asleep. I sat up and pulled the blankets over me as Crispin crawled from beneath them and hulked over as he sat cross-legged on the bed.

"Mind if I have a spliff?" He muttered groggily. The dark circles under his eyes made his eyes look bigger. I drew close to him, enjoying the warmth from his large body against mine.

I shook my head as he leaned over to crack the window and then pulled a spliff out of the side table, lighting it up. London was still cool this time of year. After Barbados, I hadn't adjusted and goosebumps prickled over my bare thighs. Crispin touched me gently and smiled.

Crispin looked sexy when he smoked, even if it was wrong for me to be attracted to his bad habits, there was something about the way his dark brows pinched together and his yellow hair fell over his face. I leaned over and kissed his cheek. He turned red. He still always turned red when I kissed him, like he was surprised that it was happening at all.

Crispin took a giant hit and the room filled with smoke. Vi liked her pills, but I preferred good old-fashioned weed once in a while. Crispin passed it over and I sighed, taking a small hit and handing it back.

"That's good," I whispered.

"Yeah… Come onto my lap, Twiggy."

I didn't need him to ask twice. I wriggled onto Crispin's lap and he wrapped his arms around me, tapping the spliff against the ash tray and then giving me a smoky kiss on my neck.

"Mm," he whispered, pushing my hair aside and kissing me. "You smell great."

His lips on my neck made everything feel okay for a bit. I could have sworn that Crispin still smelled like the beach in Barbados. I leaned back against his warmth. His body had only become more toned over time. He grabbed my waist and pulled me against him.

"Are you terribly angry with me?"

"About what?"

He'd given up on the spliff for a moment and he only gave me a look of true and genuine concern.

"We're headed back to school soon and then… summer. I don't want you to think we're breaking up," he said. "That's not what this is about."

Why the hell did he keep bringing it up? Maybe I had made him nervous about our relationship.

"We're not breaking up because you're coming to New Orleans with me," I said, trying to trick him, even if I knew it wouldn't work.

"Twiggy…" Crispin replied, his voice sounding sad. I hated hearing him sound like that, because it made his plans for the summer seem more real. And more threatening. Like he knew something he didn't want to tell me.

Crispin buried his nose in my neck again and then his voice grew strained and hoarse.

"Don't ruin it," I whispered. "Please... Let's just... kiss or whatever."

"Or whatever," he murmured. "I like the sound of that. But kissing's nice too."

I turned around and crouched between his legs. Our eyes met and Crispin lunged for me, grabbing my body against his and then kissing me properly. We couldn't go crazy like this at school between meetings, class, uniforms, practice, the Dean's Office...

Crispin tugged on my hair and drew me closer to him as we kissed more intensely. He slipped my top off my shoulder and kissed my shoulder blade and then the next thing I knew, we were both naked and Crispin kissed his way down my stomach between my legs. He forced my legs apart and his tongue found its way between them.

He pushed me to one orgasm and then another before he licked around my thighs and kissed his way back up to my breasts. He didn't try to have sex with me. He just teased me. And played with me. I came so many times that I got *hungry*. My stomach rumbled hungrily as Crispin ran his tongue over my belly button.

"That wasn't a fart!" I blurted out.

Crispin chuckled.

"So what if it was? You're allowed to toot."

OMG. No! I was *not* allowed to toot with Crispin's mouth inches away from my butt. I scrambled away from him in case he got any ideas.

"I'm not *tooting*," I said. "I'm just hungry."

"That's good," he said. "It's good when you're hungry. Shall we have breakfast?"

"It's two in the morning," I said.

"Fine," Crispin said. "I'll get you a snack, we'll sleep… then we'll have breakfast."

Crispin returned with a miniature charcuterie board from the kitchen. I ate my fill and then fell asleep on his lap while he stroked my hair. Crispin was up early the second he suspected the Fox kitchen staff would be up making breakfast preparations.

His mood always improved when breakfast entered the picture. I wanted more of him but I couldn't deny my hunger. Therapy stuff. We dressed quickly and hurried out to the kitchen at Han's Place. Ben and Libby's staff were bustling about everywhere. Kiojah and Sophie sat with Libby on the floor of their living room. She gave us a friendly greeting and the girls followed suit.

"Ben's in the kitchen having his breakfast," she said. "You're welcome to join him. I'm just trying not to let the twins break my back."

Libby patted her belly. Two sets of twins. The thought scared me out of my mind, but Libby didn't seem terrified at all. She had the most upbeat attitude. We wandered into the kitchen to find Ben sitting at the counter with his sleeves rolled up and dark circles beneath his eyes.

"Maritza, triple espresso," he snapped at one of the chefs before she bustled off with his emptied mug.

Ben barely glanced up from the paper, but his eyes fixed on Crispin.

"Barclay," he snapped. "How are you with finances?"

"Don't spend too much, listen to the money managers. I'd say I'm great."

"I'd say you are *not* great," Ben said. "Take a look at this. I've been going through the records you sent and there are massive issues. Haven't you noticed 3.7 million Euros missing from your Swiss account."

Crispin looked surprised, but barely moved considering the vast sum of money I heard him discuss like it was nothing, "Considering that's less then 1% of the total value in the Swiss account... I have *not*."

Crispin glanced at me nervously. *White boy, what*?! I wasn't an expert at math, but that meant that *one* of Crispin's accounts had over $300 million in it. He shoved his hands in his pockets uncomfortably as Ben's pen trailed across the paper.

"You've got a problem, Barclay."

"Great. Another problem. It's just money. As long as there's some left, who cares."

"Who cares?!" Ben snarled. "I spent all night divining this."

Ben jabbed an irritated finger into the paper, his cheeks turning flush.

Libby called from the living room, "Calm down, Benjamin!"

Ben raked his fingers through his golden brown hair and then sighed.

"You aren't going to like what I propose, Barclay. What are your summer plans?"

"I'm finalizing the house for Amina and... other expenses."

"Finalize them quickly. We'll talk once you're back at

college," Ben said sternly. Then he made a surprisingly Scottish sounding noise in his throat like an "och" or an "ach" and glanced around the corner impatiently searching for his espresso.

Ben's espresso returned shortly with an agitated Maritza, and Libby sauntered into the kitchen, apologizing for Ben's sullen attitude and giving him a sharp word. Ben grunted apologetically, kissing her and wrapping his arms around her waist as he gulped his coffee down. Libby pinched her husband's stubble covered cheeks and prodded him into conversation eventually. But Crispin's attitude soured as Libby improved Ben's. Money problems. The more money you had, the bigger and weirder the problems. Crispin hated talking about money. I didn't see the point in talking about it but I suddenly wondered about his money and what he *felt* about it. He was rich.

Not even John Hewett had $300 million. Crispin was really, really rich. And there was another secret — one that Crispin probably didn't even know yet — and it was buried somewhere in his millions.

Chapter Twenty-Seven

Vi returned from Easter break with a deep tan that matched Jack Dyson's. When they arrived on campus together with Vi's naturally sun bleached hair and Dyson's tanned musculature, everyone talked about how amazing they looked. Over the holiday, Vi appeared to have made some headway in Jack's personal grooming routine and his fingernails were clean — a small, but impressive accomplishment. She loved Hong Kong, but found Jack Dyson's family insufferable.

"He has as many brothers as I do," she complained.

The Dyson's and the Bainbridge's were both renowned for their feral bands of brothers. Poor Vi. The school's biggest feminist always seemed to find herself surrounded by rowdy men.

Our year couldn't stop buzzing about the latest departures from campus. Rumors spread that Katrina Grigsby's medical leave had been because she contracted sleeping sickness from a tsetse fly while on vacation to Gabon — a rumor as detailed as it was false. Gossiping Year 12s blamed Ella

Novak's departure on her parents' bankruptcy which everyone knew about now because they owned one of the largest apartment buildings in Central London which had recently been foreclosed in a public manner. Her campus relationships broke apart and Trevor claimed she was "moving to America" which everyone agreed was far too unlikely to be true. Trevor had recently also announced his vow of celibacy to the entire year, if for no other reason than to ensure he was the center of *some* new controversy.

Group chats broke up and stitched back together over the holiday and by the time I arrived back on campus with Crispin, I was in an entirely new group chat: Mandy, Vi, Sarah Clifford and Julia. Julia was more Mandy's friend, but she was cool.

MANDY: Urgent meeting. Boy advice needed.
Vi: Which boy?

WE CONVENED IN OUR ROOM. Mandy made tea as she paced nervously in a black turtleneck and matching leggings. Her mother-of-pearl Van Cleef and Arpels necklace hung off center around her neck. She straightened it nervously. Mandy's red birthmark got slightly darker when she was upset and the marking covered most of the area beneath her left eye like it had been splatter painted on.

Her hair draped over her shoulders and she whittled her fingernails down to stubs as we unpacked our clothes from the Easter break together.

"You should invite Crispin," Mandy said seriously.

"Why? This is girl talk. He can mind his tall boy business."

Mandy didn't respond. She set out little mugs (she had a massive collection) and added a tea bag to each one in anticipation of our girl gang assembly. Vi arrived first, red-faced and complaining about Jack. He'd stolen one of her thongs and hung it up in his gym locker. Mandy eagerly embraced the conversational distraction until the rest of the group assembled. Julia sat at Mandy's desk, her strawberry blond hair tied back in a kerchief as she sipped the tea Mandy poured her. Sarah Clifford arrived next, apologizing for her lateness and dragged along Paige Rapetti from down the hall.

"Paige, you're welcome to come, have my mug," Mandy said.

"Okay," Vi said. "What's wrong. Boy problem."

The energy in the room was heightened and a little excited. We were all ready for the pending Easter break.

"I had sex," Mandy announced. "For the first time."

The room erupted into squeals.

"When!?" Sarah asked excitedly.

"Wait, has everyone here done it?" Vi said next, scanning the room like she was conducting an Arthur Miller style witch hunt for virgins.

Julia was the only one who hadn't and her cheeks flushed red as she lamented, "Great. I'm the only virgin."

"Answer the question," Sarah pressed.

"For break I was in London and... we sort of... ran into each other."

"Who?!" I said.

The suspense was killing me. *Killing me.*

"Wait, don't answer that yet," Sarah said. "Tell us all the details and then we'll guess? Or maybe we'll guess first!"

Sarah sounded like she was guessing the most important fact in the universe. Vi was all the way locked in to the gossip too.

"Is he older?" Vi asked enthusiastically.

"No," Mandy said. "He goes to our school."

A sudden terrifying thought seized me.

"Omg. Is it Devin!?"

She said he was sexy, right? Maybe she'd taken the plunge... But Mandy's birthmark only darkened and she shook her head.

"Not Devin," she answered solemnly.

"How was it?" Sarah Clifford asked eagerly. "Details."

"It was... at my parents' hotel. They said I could use the penthouse for the holiday and he sort of... came over... one thing led to another and... we had sex."

"Did you orgasm?" Vi asked with complete seriousness.

Mandy nodded and whispered, "Several times..."

I yelled out, "Who?"

"Okay, you can't judge me. He doesn't want me telling anyone on campus."

"Who cares what he wants?" Sarah pressed, fiercely staring at Mandy with the passion of someone about to update Trevor in the group chat. "*Tell us.*"

For once, I agreed with Sarah Clifford.

"Kaito Cammish," Mandy said.

I felt like an idiot. *Duh.* I had seen them dancing at the party and getting all close to each other, but I had been so wrapped up in my own mess I forgot. Because I'd seen them, my reaction wasn't the most dramatic.

"WHAT?!" Vi yelled, jumping to her feet, taking up the mantle of adding her high energy to the situation. The other girls screeched and Mandy buried her head in her hands, her hair falling around her face and she groaned.

"I know. I know. I told myself I wasn't going to let him come over. I'm a terrible friend."

"He *burned me*," Vi snapped. "He's a complete *arsehole*."

"I know what he did to you was wrong but... he's not like that anymore."

"I think he is like that," I muttered.

Vi turned on me next. "Oh, you're one to talk..."

"What does that mean?" I said defensively, although I was smart enough to figure out what Vi meant. Since when was I under attack here?

"Everyone knows Crispin's a sociopath," Vi grumbled.

"Vi," Mandy said. "That's not fair. Crispin's not a sociopath and he didn't kill his parents."

"Jack Dyson can't even keep his nails clean," I said. "I'll take a sociopath over a guy with no hygiene."

Vi huffed, but she couldn't disagree. Mandy glanced nervously at Vi, uncertain of what to say next.

Before the conversation could descend into the pits of hell, Sarah Clifford yelled, "LADIES! We are talking about boys. At the end of the day, they're all arseholes. Can we just agree to let each other have our arseholes?!"

"I find it hard to believe Kaito's good in bed," Vi grumbled, unable to let herself go without one last retort. It just rolled off of Mandy who was far too distressed about losing her virginity to the year's biggest sociopath.

Mandy sighed.

"So did I. But he was... You can't tell anyone, okay?"

"We won't," Sarah assured her. "But why doesn't he want you to tell people?"

"He's ashamed," Julia said. "It might ruin his reputation."

"Thanks…" Mandy grumbled.

Julia didn't mean to be an asshole, but she sounded like one when she said, "I mean… he sort of plays the field, doesn't he?"

"He's not like that," Mandy insisted. "He gets what it's like to be Asian. Whatever. You wouldn't understand."

She flopped back on her bed and dragged her pillow onto her head and we all felt bad for a bit. Here Mandy was telling us about her good dick and we just couldn't get past the fact that it was about Kaito Cammish.

"So are you dating him?" I asked.

"I dunno. He probably has summer plans. So no."

"Summer plans. Who has summer plans?" Vi said.

"I do."

Everyone turned to look at me.

"With Crispin?"

"Yeah," I said. "But you all can come. We should book flights together. I'm spending the summer in New Orleans."

"New Orleans?" Vi said curiously. "Is that close to New York?"

"No," I said. "It's where I'm from… originally. Before I was adopted."

"You're adopted?" Julia said. "That's so cool."

At least she didn't ask if my parents "saved me from Africa" like half the people I'd met.

"I'm going to research my birth parents," I said. "I'll be basically getting my hot girl summer on at the pool and learning about New Orleans I guess."

"Can we go to Mardi Gras?" Sarah asked.

I explained that I didn't think it was in the summer, but then everyone talked about what they knew about New Orleans. Mandy was excited by the prospect too.

"I'm tired of spending all my summers in the penthouse watching television. My parents don't like me going out without escorts in London and it's *awful*."

"Not to mention we can spare you the temptation of inviting Kaito Cammish over," Vi grumbled.

Mandy sighed.

"He's probably a twat," she said sadly.

"Definitely a twat," Sarah agreed. "We should have a summer with no boys."

"Except Crispin," Mandy said. "He's Amina's boyfriend so he's like... important to the mission."

"No boys except Crispin," Vi said eagerly. "That sounds like a perfect summer."

"What about Jack?" I asked, but Vi didn't get a chance to respond.

MY PHONE BUZZED and I glanced down at it. My heart always did this funny jump when I saw his name. It flipped twice as hard when I read the message.

Crispin: we need to talk.

Chapter Twenty-Eight

I met Crispin in his bedroom. Devin was back in the dorms but he'd moved to another room. I was surprised to find him and Crispin studying together when I came in through the window to Crispin's new dorm room.

"Devin?"

I was about to go off on him when Crispin sat up from his bed, distracting me. The look on his face was pure... anguish.

"We'll continue this later, McLeod," he said brusquely and Devin gave him a thump on the back before leaving immediately at Crispin's command. Devin winced as he lurched forward, still healing from the wound Crispin inflicted on his abdomen from the stabbing. Devin appeared to be in good spirits and he showed everyone who asked (and several people who didn't ask) his healing wound.

"You two are still friends?" I asked bitterly once he'd successfully banished the redhead.

"We're not going to get a little stabbing get between us.

We're both vying for team captain next year," Crispin said calmly.

"Is that done by election?"

"It's happening now by election," Crispin said. "Coach will announce it tomorrow."

"Do you want it?"

"Of course I do," Crispin said. "But I'm... not as likable as Devin."

I found *that* hard to believe. Crispin grabbed my shoulders, rubbing them slowly, and I got the distinct sense that he hadn't texted me to complain about soccer captain elections.

"What's wrong?"

"Ben called. I finished all the transactions and... the house is yours. You've got a little money but... Ben thinks we need to freeze the accounts for the summer and he's hiring a forensic accountant to look into things. I won't have... *money* for the next 6 months."

"What do you mean you won't have money?"

"Ben loaned me a little bit of spending money for the summer but... I'll have to work I suppose."

"Like an internship?"

Crispin shrugged. "I dunno. Something that pays like... $250 an hour might get me where I need."

I pursed my lips into a thin line. Crispin was in trouble, wasn't he? Mathematically, that made absolutely no sense and the longer he considered the math, the more I could tell he had no idea what was going to happen to him or his finances with the frozen accounts.

I wrapped my arms around him tightly, squeezing him. He hugged back, kissing my head.

"What's that for?" I asked, leaning into Crispin's hug. Leaving him would hurt so much, I didn't know if I could handle it. I already felt like someone was strangling me and we hadn't even separated yet.

"We're going to be okay," he said. "I just want you to know that."

"I don't want you to send me away."

Crispin pinches his brow together. "I have to," he said. "America is much bigger than England and there are infinite places I could spirit you away if something went wrong."

He stopped and pushed hair out of his face. He had really thought this through.

"Why can't I just learn how to use a gun or something?" I asked. I mean, I already knew how to use a gun, but I didn't want Crispin to know that and I *was* out of practice. Plus, daddy would only let me use the 22-caliber rifle because I was so little. With a *real* weapon, I could keep myself safe.

"It's dangerous here and it's dangerous in America. No matter what, you will be protected, Amina. That's all that's important to me."

He put his hands on my waist and I was ready to forget all about money and the summer again. Crispin kissed me and when he pulled away, he sighed.

"Katrina and Freddie won't have money either. They're hiding out in Scotland for now but... I don't know how to tell them they'll be at the cottage on a... *budget*."

He said the word 'budget' like it was filled with a nest of baby roaches.

"Is that why you wanted to talk?"

"Yeah," Crispin said. "I just... wanted to see you. To feel you."

He kissed me again and I kissed back hard, pushing him against his bed. Crispin chuckled and pulled me onto him. I wanted to feel him too. We had six more weeks of school, final exams, and then summer. Before long, we'd be sleeping in the same bed and I'd wake up to Crispin's delicious breakfasts before exploring my roots.

He promised that eventually, he would come – but he couldn't give me any specific time he would be with me in America. I hated the uncertainty. I also hated the thought of trying to discover my roots without Crispin, who understood everything about me.

I didn't know anything about my roots or what that even meant.

Crispin's hair fell out of its messy bun. The longer his hair got, the more frustrated Crispin became. He fought it back into the bun with a scowl on his face, tugging at the skin on his cheekbones as he wrapped his blond hair around itself and it immediately fell out of his grasp.

"It's too long," he groaned, finally wrestling his hair back into a knot. I loved his hair and didn't find it frustrating at all.

"Why don't you cut it?"

"Lazy," he whispered, running his hands over my butt. "I'd rather make love to my girl…"

I struggled against his chest and got my fingers through his hair.

"I like it," I whispered.

"You've mentioned."

"You can cut it in the summer," I whispered. "When we're together."

Crispin's brow furrowed and he nodded.

233

"Is there something else going on?" I asked. Crispin shook his head.

"Are you sure?"

He insisted nothing was wrong. I tugged at his shirt and Crispin's demeanor softened.

"Brilliant," he murmured. "Have at me, Twiggy."

I didn't need him to tell me twice. I stripped Crispin's shirt off and just *touched* him. He liked when I touched him like this. He squirmed and moved beneath my touch until he was ready to strip my clothes off. Crispin peeled my clothing off one slow movement at a time. First my shirt slid off his bed and he slipped my bra off my shoulders before his tongue found my breasts and he teased me slowly. I moaned as his tongue roamed over my nipple and then we both heard shuffling outside the door.

"Fuck's sake," Crispin murmured, hiking my legs around him and then glaring at the door.

He kissed me and I grabbed his face, stopping him.

"Didn't you hear that?"

Crispin nodded, murmuring and continuing to kiss me. There was more shuffling outside the door.

"Fuck off, Devin!" Crispin yelled.

"Sorry…"

I wriggled against him and Crispin sighed.

"Sorry. He's a pervert."

We didn't dwell on Devin. Crispin was hard and I didn't care what Devin was up to. I just wanted Crispin now and for the rest of the summer. I didn't care if he had money and I didn't care about forensic accountants or anything except us ending up together. Crispin tugged at the waist of my underwear, but didn't yank it off.

"I want to taste you," he whispered, touching my stomach and then kissing my neck. "But... you have a C- in history... so I think we'd better study."

I wanted to *kill* him. I scowled and tried to fight but Crispin only chuckled.

"Only joking, Twiggy. I can taste you first, then we'll talk about Henry VI."

Crispin's love of English history had to be a form of mental illness. I scowled and tried to distract him with something way sexier than an English king.

"Or we can never talk about Henry VI again and have sex," I said. "All night."

"One hour of sex... two hours of studying. Deal or no deal," he murmured, running his hand along my cheek and then caressing my stomach with his firm hands. Crispin's touch could convince me of anything.

"Fine," I whispered, ignoring the part where I had to study. I could just convince Crispin not to study later.

He grabbed my arms and pinned them over my head, slowly angling them there and then pressing down on me with just enough force that I could anticipate what was coming. With wide eyes and eager squirming hips, my gaze met his.

Crispin glanced over me with bewitching blue eyes. Even now, he didn't have an interest in rushing. He slowly spread my legs apart and touched only my inner thighs with a wide palm.

"Now," he whispered, the corners of his mouth turning up into a lust-filled smirk. "I'm going to make you cum and you're going to make sure that no one in this dormitory hears a sound. Think you can handle that, Lips?"

He knew it would be a struggle for me, but he only grinned mischievously as his hand tickled the inside of my thigh and I struggled to stifle a moan. I nodded and Crispin spread my thighs with his hands, still grinning as he pushed his fingers softly between my spread lower lips. We both groaned as he found me soaked and slipped inside me.

"There," he whispered. "You're perfect, Amina."

I arched my hips up as he pushed inside me again. I moaned and Crispin's free hand darted over my mouth. He bent his lips to my neck and kissed me again before he whispered, "Quiet, Lips. Please…"

His fingers moved out of me and his hands slipped and slid to the most sensitive parts of me. Crispin always knew exactly where to touch. Using his hands, he massaged me until I was so close to cumming I thought I'd burst. When I bucked my hips up one last time he withdrew and I sank into his bed with a desperate gasp. I wanted more.

Crispin hadn't finished. He greedily kissed his way down the length of my stomach and then he spread my lower lips apart with his tongue. Crispin's perpetual hunger only exploded between my legs. He spread my lower lips with an agile tongue and fixated on my clit, bringing me to the edge of an intense climax and then finally gripping my thighs and pushing me over the edge with his tongue and fingers.

My sticky thighs and sweat-covered body contorted and twisted with pleasure as I stifled my moans but accepted each new orgasm with growing desire for more as Crispin never grew tired of kissing my pussy and then bringing me to the edge with his enthusiastic tongue. I lost track of how much I came. But damn… it was good. I didn't want to leave Crispin's bed even for a moment.

Just when I planned to roll over and fall asleep, Crispin drew me to him, resting his hand between my quivering thighs.

"Now," Crispin whispered. "Study time."

Had it been an hour already?

Chapter Twenty-Nine

S tudying. Sex. Studying. Sex. We continued like that until morning with only a few hours of sleep. We both went to classes exhausted, but I actually knew some of the answers when our history teacher called on me. That was a nice change. I had to get at least a B+ on the final exam otherwise Agatha would have my head.

For two weeks, school continued as it usually did. I studied as much as I could and Crispin helped me whenever he was free. I even helped Devin give Crispin a shaggy hair cut before the summer because he'd threatened to shave his head. When I was in my room, Mandy was in full meltdown mode over her studies. Her father wasn't pleased that she had a B- in mathematics and she drilled herself with militaristic enthusiasm to improve her grade on the final exam.

"I really want him to let me go to America," she explained to me.

Her parents didn't like her doing non-traditional things, but they'd let her out of their sight if she was with friends. I wondered what would happen with her and Kaito, but she hadn't mentioned him since her confession.

In the evenings, I'd sneak out to Crispin's room and we'd repeat our nightly routine. Studying. Sex. Final exams had all of campus stressed out and even Vi was sneaking over to Jack Dyson's room for stress relief of her own.

One week before finals, Crispin surprised me by canceling our study session.

Me: tomorrow?

Crispin: yes, sweetheart.

Me: everything ok?

Crispin: Ben's worried.

CRISPIN COULD BE ODDLY cryptic like that. We'd talk tomorrow he'd said. Since he mentioned Ben, this probably had to do with his parents and his continued investigation into the mysterious black hard drive that Freddie lost the night they died. Crispin hadn't mentioned Freddie in a week or two. She was in Scotland with Katrina, but that was about it.

Katrina finally sent Vi pictures of her baby bump, keeping her under strict directives not to share the photos with anyone else. I thought it would be a miracle if Katrina pulled off keeping this secret but so far, no one guessed the real reason she left. Rapetti's Christian club missed her dearly, but aside from that, more people cared about exams than gossiping about Katrina Grigsby anymore.

I got ready to study in bed since Crispin canceled on me.

Mandy had gone to the library an hour earlier armed with bags full of candy and energy drinks. She probably wouldn't get back until dorm check-in. I studied history in bed for a while and when my eyes glazed over, I threw my hair up into a crazy looking messy bun and reviewed the outline for my English essay. I was feeling like a girl boss when Vi texted asking to come over and study.

When Vi came over, I was grateful that she had dutifully taken crazy-detailed notes in all our classes. Why wasn't *she* valedictorian? I couldn't tell why not because her notes were insanely good. Better than Crispin's. He'd just go on about remembering the lectures and he remembered them in specific detail. We studied until Mandy returned and then the three of us studied together. Vi had special permission to be in our dorm for the night. Mandy and I pushed our beds together and the three of us climbed in, falling asleep together with our papers surrounding us.

I didn't have a good reason for it, but I spent the night tossing and turning. Mandy and Vi slept like logs, unlike Crispin, so they hardly noticed how sleepless my night was. I woke up at 4 a.m. feeling and looking like a bug eyed zombie. I checked my weight in the bathroom instinctively, noticing how it made me feel to step on a scale. 1lb up. I'd done it. I was still at a healthy weight.

Grinning like I never expected to, I glanced at my face in the bathroom mirror and I was grateful that black didn't crack one bit because the bags under my eyes would have looked severe if I'd been as pale as Crispin. My smile vanished. He hadn't texted me back in hours. This wasn't like him. I wanted to tell him the good news about my weight on top of everything else.

.   .   .

ME: hey, white boy.

HE DIDN'T REPLY. Crispin was usually awake. Seriously, he'd message back quickly no matter the time of day. I guessed he'd been studying all night and didn't get my message.

ME: can't sleep.

No REPLY. Sigh. I guess I'd go over there. Since Crispin lived alone now for "medical reasons", I could sneak in through his window without worrying about his goofy red-headed ex-roommate. It was nearly summer, but still cool outside. I slipped into black leggings and one of Crispin's hoodies. I found half a cigarette in the little pocket as I stuck my hands in and tossed it out as I snuck outside and hugged the walls of the dorm so I could get to the boys' dorm without anyone noticing me.

It was early in the morning, so I could always pretend I was going on a stress-induced early morning run. The rules were lax around exams because students were so stressed. There'd already been a stabbing on campus (thanks, Crispin) so something small like sneaking out was unlikely to get me into *really* hot water.

I approached Crispin's window and found it cracked. I shook my head.

There was a little jump from the ground, but it almost looked like Crispin had just snuck out of his bedroom.

"Crispin!" I hissed.

He didn't reply. Great. He probably had his headphones on or something and couldn't hear me. That didn't explain why he didn't answer his phone, but with the open window at least I could climb in. I just hoped I wouldn't land in an awkward pile of limbs like I normally did when I climbed in alone. Using the cuff of Crispin's giant sweatshirt to help me grip. I grabbed onto the ledge and stuck my foot on one of the bricks jutting out slightly beneath his window.

I wobbled, but maintained my grasp as I used every ounce of upper body strength to drag me up to the window. I called his name through my grunting as I dragged myself up.

The first thing that hit me was that Crispin's room smelled *terribly*.

I landed through the window and then slipped in something that felt like melted jello. I slipped forward, landing against the wall instead of the floor. His bedroom was still dark. What the hell did I just step in? Instinctively, I reached for the floor lamp closest to Crispin's bed and turned it on.

The flash of light illuminated a horrifying scene and my instincts took over.

I couldn't stop myself from screaming. The ungodly shriek that came out of my mouth brought me right back to the night I found August Barclay dead. His brother's limbs were now contorted in the same ghastly fashion and there was blood. What I'd just stepped in had been Crispin's blood. His room smelled like flesh and metal. I screamed louder.

More blood than I'd ever seen in my life. I panicked and I dropped to my knees, continuing to scream. Crispin and his floor were both covered in blood and my boyfriend appeared to be very dead.

I didn't care about the blood. It was all over me anyway and soaking through my clothes. I screamed his name. I could hear shuffling in the hallway as I shrieked. I had to touch him. I had to make sure that he wasn't cold. I didn't stop screaming as I sank to the floor next to him and took Crispin's limp hand in mine.

Chapter Thirty

My black cardigan wrapped around me. I wanted to feel something. Anything. But I was numb. Vi put her arms around my shoulder.

"He's not dead," she whispered. "He'll be fine."

Mandy wrapped her arms around me, her eyes watering. She'd been crying as much as I had. But I just couldn't cry anymore. Police arrived on campus and everything happened so quickly. They took Crispin from me and the police held me back for questioning instead of letting me ride with him in the ambulance. Vi wouldn't let me talk to them without a lawyer and she had her dad on the phone to send one within five minutes of the cops showing up.

Now all that was done and Dean Leonard had given us special permission to come to the hospital. Mandy borrowed Kaito's car keys and Violet drove us to the hospital, trying to fight back tears of her own. We didn't actually know that Crispin wasn't dead. When I'd touched his hand... I couldn't tell. Or I couldn't remember.

Or I wanted him to be alive when he wasn't. The thought

settled like a wiry pit in my stomach, scraping the edges of my insides and rubbing me raw. Nearly everyone in Crispin's family had been killed and clearly, he was next. I felt like the sound I made hadn't come from my mouth, that it was someone else crying.

"He's strong," Mandy whispered. "He'll make it."

WE ENTERED THE HOSPITAL TOGETHER, lined up like we were a small army of college students. It was so cold. I hated it. Mandy put her arm around me, but it didn't help. *This was going to hurt.* I didn't want anything to happen to Crispin, but something had already happened to him. I hated hospitals.

A nurse emerged from the operating theater with an unreadable expression on her face. Nurses and doctors have that expressionless face mastered, which almost makes it seem like they enjoy taunting you with the uncertainty. Violet's hand slipped into mine.

"Are you his sister?" She said to Violet.

"His friend," Vi said. "This is his girlfriend and we're friends."

"We need to wait for a blood relative."

Mercifully, a voice came from behind me that sent all the relief in the world flooding through me.

"I'm here. I drove here as soon as I could."

Freddie towered over Katrina, who stood beside her with a now obvious baby bump. Katrina wore a pink wig, but otherwise modest clothing. Freddie dressed in all black. I had to admit, her clothes were cool. Her black boots elevated her even taller than before and her wide legged pants cinched at a pale, thin waist. Freddie wore black liner and a scowl that looked exactly like Crispin's except for Freddie's entirely different features.

The nurse asked for identification and Freddie reluctantly withdrew hers. Katrina sidled up to her and nearly ignored Violet and Mandy.

"Katrina," Vi said. "How are you?"

Katrina grimaced uncomfortably.

"I'm fine. Getting fat. But whatever."

"I *know* you're pregnant," Vi said.

Katrina glared at Mandy.

"But *she* didn't," Katrina said, as if it were Mandy's fault for existing. Vi stepped in front of Mandy and folded her arms.

"Everyone can tell you're pregnant Katrina," Vi said with frustration. "I just wanted to know how you've been."

"Fine. I'm praying. Dying my hair. Relaxing. It's pregnancy and I'm stuck with a psychopathic goth prison guard. It's not exactly perfect."

Freddie shot Katrina a glare and continued speaking to the nurse in hushed tones. Vi sighed and rolled her eyes.

"Whatever. But don't be rude to Mandy."

Katrina rolled her eyes.

"You're the one who has a new best friend."

"That's not true. You're still my best friend. I just want to know more. I want to be there for you."

"No one wants to be there for me," Katrina snapped.

Before Vi could say anything else, Freddie turned away from the nurse.

"Amina?" She said. "I've asked and you can come in with me to see him."

Tears welled in her eyes, a break from the tough girl character draped in black before me. Freddie slipped her hand in mine, an oddly intimate gesture. It occurred to me that she was doing this because the news was horrible. Crispin. Dead. My stomach churned and I couldn't make myself take a single step forward. Freddie braced and stopped walking.

"You're shaking," she said.

"Yeah."

"You love him, don't you?"

Love him? Yes, I loved Crispin. We were going to spend the summer together... We were supposed to be together *forever*.

I never dreamed about getting married or having romance in my life because of what happened to me. I thought I was broken. I thought I could just hook up with guys like Devin until one decided to settle down. I never thought the boy I'd fall in love with would be Crispin.

I hadn't liked him at first. He'd been too beautiful. Too alluring. And I hated that everyone paid attention to him because it reminded me of Daddy, really. Always at the center of a media something.

"Yes," I whispered to Freddie, squeezing her hand.

"If you love him, you have to know that he'll pull through."

"I don't understand who would hurt him like this?"

I didn't even know what happened. There was just blood. And pain.

FREDDIE DIDN'T ANSWER. She pulled me along with her another step and then the nurses opened Crispin's hospital room. I froze as two security guards flanked the doors. Freddie's grasp on my hand tightened.

"Sorry, Amina," she whispered. "I had to get them."

The nurse approached both of us with a grim expression on her face.

"We don't know how long he has."

"How long?" My heart thudded in my chest. This was it. The first and only boy I'd ever loved was going to die right in front of me.

"He's awake," she said. "But he only keeps his eyes open for a moment or two. You won't get much out of him and he ought to rest."

I approached the bed and my stomach lurched as I drew closer to Crispin's enormous body. His chest rose and then sank with a slow breath. Not a dying breath, I told myself, just a slow breath.

"Crispin," I whispered. I missed using his name. I'd call him boy or white boy, but I hardly ever called him Crispin. It was a soft name that always sounded like a whisper and seemed fitting for a boy who didn't like attention. It wasn't his fault he'd grown up to become the center of it.

Freddie could almost read my mind.

"Someone already leaked the news."

Crispin groaned and I didn't wait for Freddie to say anything else. I rushed toward him and then noticed the bandages over his eyes, which had been covered up by the blanket and the dark shadows in his room. I touched his hand, so at least he'd know it was me.

"Crispin," I whispered. "It's me. It's Amina. I'm right here…"

Freddie sniffled, but she didn't get any closer to the bed. I examined Crispin as best I could for injuries. He was covered in bandages but the ones that worried me most were the ones around his eyes. I hadn't noticed anything when I found him because his eyes had been closed.

What the hell happened?

I didn't want to leave him, but I knew I'd have to go if I couldn't even get him to wake up enough to say a word.

"Crispin," I whispered again. "I love you. I'm right here and I love you. Please, white boy... don't die on me."

Chapter Thirty-One

I dutifully trekked over to Jack Dyson's Land Rover after class to find Vi sitting on the hood of the car, her legs wrapped around Jack's body as they kissed passionately. Jack kissed her with so much eagerness, I thought he'd eat her face. Vi for once, wasn't screaming at him. She tangled her fingers in his long messy hair and giggled as he pulled away to hand her a tangerine from his pocket. This particular fruit was unblemished and not even rotten. Wow.

I was envious, even if I was also disgusted with myself for the sudden inappropriate surge of feeling. Not because of Jack, but because they could be a proper couple. They could be with each other. Crispin and I wouldn't have that as long as he was in recovery. He'd barely said ten words since waking up and he'd barely spent any time at all awake. This was serious.

At least he was alive. Even that sounded like something you'd say about an office plant. I wanted more than his survival. I needed to know he would be himself again – that he could be Crispin. My backpack nearly dragged me to the ground. Using as much threatening language as I could, I convinced Devin to help me get Crispin's books and assignments to bring to the hospital with him.

I'd been heading over to study for the past three weeks. I got a lot done when he slept and whenever he woke up, he'd silently quiz me with flashcards and try to get me to talk about everything except his injuries and who could have possibly hurt him and left him for dead on Rapetti's campus. Katrina and Freddie were at the cottage, but so far my attempts to avoid Katrina involved avoiding Freddie too. I knew he must have had a good reason for his silence, but I hated the feeling that he was keeping a secret from me. *What didn't he want me to know?*

Jack pulled away from Vi, slowly tugging on her lower lip between his as she jumped off the hood of his Land Rover and the smile from her face fell, replaced with worry. I hated to make Violet worry.

"Where's Mandy?"

"She isn't coming today," I said. "She has a meeting over her French grades."

"Ouch."

"Care for a tangerine, Amina?" Jack said slowly, reaching for one in his pocket that looked about a week old. He dramatically pulled lint off it and blew it clean, spraying it with his saliva in the process.

"No thanks," I said, smiling at him appreciatively. Vi cast a knowing look in my direction and tucked brown hair behind her ears.

"We'd better go see him then," she said, casting a sympathetic glance in my direction.

I always got quiet on the drives to the hospital. I'd think

about finding Crispin in his blood and the way his injuries still looked. I'd think about losing him. I'd think about his pain and how he could endure so much of it.

How could he be so crazy as to think we should spend the summer apart? I needed to look after him as much as he needed to look after me. Today, we'd have to have a heart to heart and figure it all out. I had a great plan too. Crispin would just have to listen to me. I was all dressed for success. I wasn't even wearing black. I wore white. Uh huh. I thought it might cheer Crispin up. He hated the hospital. Sigh. Vi commented on how cute my dress was. I didn't have the heart to tell her that I borrowed it from Mandy, who was my new size.

I managed to eat by making some messed up mental bargain that I was convinced would work. If I ate, I would bring Crispin back. Hey, it worked most of the time.

When we arrived at the hospital, Jack and Vi stopped into Crispin's room with me at first like they usually did. I unpacked my stuff, history books, Crispin's annotated copy of *Macbeth*, and then my graphing calculator, and sat at the foot of Crispin's bed. Today, he was in a great mood.

"The food's rubbish," he snarled impetuously. "I asked for haddock and they brought me rubber. I can't believe this is *private* health care. I can't sit here. I ought to be at home."

Vi glanced at Jack, who cleared his throat.

Crispin didn't wait for a response before continuing. "They wash with this *white* soap. What was in that thing? No goat milk. No grapefruit zest. Just a *soap*. I thought sponge bath was a figure of speech."

"Listen, mate. If you'd like, we can hire chefs and stuff to feed you and erm... perhaps Amina can wash your bollocks.

But you've got to eat. I've noticed you're getting a bit thin. You're the team Captain now. You have to be strong."

Crispin scowled fiercely.

"Yes," he said. "I'm wasting away. I want to get out of here. I want to wash my own bollocks for a change."

Jack was no good at calming Crispin down. I stepped in front of him, folding my arms and pretending not to notice Crispin staring intently at my outfit.

"You can't get out of bed, white boy," I said. "Just be happy you can do virtual exams and once they're over, we can go back to the countryside and chill together."

His hands found mine, his index finger nervously scraping at my palm.

"Thanks, babe."

Jack and Vi excused themselves for the rest of the afternoon. Vi normally went shopping with Jack as her official bag-carrier to reduce her study stress. I was pretty sure she was responsible for cleaning out the nearest boutiques in a ten mile radius for all their designer items. Her room was packed with white bags and receipts.

Once we were alone, Crispin's relative cheeriness descended into outright gloom. He hadn't stopped holding my hand.

"How many have you had so far?" He asked patiently. He always inquired after school — and insisted upon doing so — before talking about his injuries. But that was all I wanted to talk about. Someone had nearly taken Crispin Barclay from me and I wanted blood.

"Four," I said impatiently. "I've got two more exams."

"Perfect. How'd they go?"

We'd had this conversation before. But with his concussion, we had some of the same conversations several times before Crispin could remember. His head was still wrapped up in bandages.

"They went well," I said, but how the hell did I know. I always thought my exams went well until I got my grades back.

"You don't want to talk about exams."

How could I? I shook my head. Crispin sighed.

"I'm sorry."

"Someone attacked you. I leave here and I don't know if it's the last time I'm going to see you."

"I'm right here. I'm alive."

"Why won't you explain anything to me?!"

"Darling... I don't remember. I was unconscious."

"Someone attacked you. In case you've forgotten, you're 6'6" and you could crush Godzilla's neck with a squeeze. You *must* know who did it. I blamed Devin at first, you know. I tried to get revenge on him."

Crispin grinned.

"What did you do to the redhead?"

"Don't worry about it," I grumbled, swiftly avoiding Crispin changing the subject. Again. Devin had it coming. And anyway, his hair would grow back.

"Right." His hand gripped mine protectively. "I don't know who attacked me. I'm serious."

"Does Ben know? What about Theo? I thought they were helping you and now they've gone and left you for dead."

I'd been surprised that Crispin didn't have his friend or his cousin visit him yet. His lips pursed into a thin line. Then I heard a voice behind me.

"Yes, Ben knows. And Barclay appears rather *lively* today."

I turned around to meet Benjamin Fox's gaze. His eyes were freakishly green, but he smiled when he saw me. It was strange seeing him without Libby by his side. She softened his appearance. Now, in Crispin's hospital room he appeared cold and threatening.

"Hello, Amina," Ben said. I stumbled backward, my butt pressed against Crispin's bed. Crispin squeezed my hand tighter. Theo appeared in the doorway behind his best friend. The Rapetti graduates were nearly the same height, but Theo's features were soft and angelic compared to Ben's gruff caveman look.

"Hello, Amina," Theo said, waving at me, his eyes eerily similar to my boyfriend's but the rest of him lean and wiry where Crispin was broad and muscular. They didn't greet Crispin and he didn't meet their gaze. Or mine.

"How long have you been here?" I asked them suspicious.

Crispin squeezed my hand again.

"Stay strong, Amina," he whispered. "Please. I'm really sorry, but I need you to be safe."

Ben raised his right eyebrow.

"Did you tell her?" He asked.

Crispin's lips pursed and I wrestled my hand away from him.

"Tell me what? What's going on?"

They were blocking the door. Noticing that sent a surge of panic coursing through me. I'd been in situations like this before — situations where I needed to escape. If I couldn't push through them, I could always kick and scream my way out.

"It's better you hate me than him," Ben said, crossing the room and closing his hand around my wrist. I tried to pull away, but Ben only tightened his grasp and he was powerful.

Theo said, "I'm really sorry."

Then he took my other hand. I tried to yank my arms away from both of them. Crispin still wouldn't look at me and I found myself powerlessly suspended between two of my boyfriend's best friends. I'd trusted him. I'd trusted all of them.

Ben made a weak attempt to reassure me. "I promise, we will not hurt you. We're doing this for your own good. Trust Barclay."

I turned around madly, but Crispin wouldn't meet my gaze. I made a loud grunting noise and used all my strength to try to pull away from Ben and Theo.

"Crispin? What's going on?"

Crispin didn't answer me.

"Dyson and Bainbridge will return in thirty minutes," Crispin said calmly. "I'll explain to them once you have her out of here."

This was his plan.

"LET GO OF ME!" I screamed, interrupting them. Ben turned a cold expression onto Crispin.

"It would have been better if you'd told her," Ben snapped at him before returning his gaze to me. "Come on, Amina."

"I'm not going anywhere with you. Where's Libby?"

"Preoccupied," Ben said. "And the easier you make this on me, the more likely I am *not* to miss the birth of my biological children so please, Amina Hewett, don't fight this."

I fought. Naturally. Ben and Theo dragged me out of the hospital kicking and screaming. Lots of screaming. I got up onto Ben's shoulders at one point and attempted to leap away to safety, only to land in Theo's arms. He was stronger than he looked — apparently, also a rugby player — and he tossed me over his shoulder as I yelled.

Kidnapped. My boyfriend's having me kidnapped. I screamed bloody murder throughout the hospital as the nurses turned to their work and ignored everything happening around them. I was being kidnapped and no one was doing anything to help.

I told Crispin that I hated him and I bit Theo's shoulder and tried to climb out the window. The drive was hell. I fought the entire way until Ben pulled his car over to a tiny airstrip with a luxurious private jet. He double checked the locks on the doors as he stopped and his tense shoulders relaxed slightly. He turned to his best friend.

"Theo. You'll take good care of her? Libby will *murder me* when she finds out. You'll have to step in and donate all your money to the twins to support them once I've perished."

He paused uncomfortably and sighed. Ben didn't want to do this. Great. But that hadn't stopped him from this orchestrating this stupid plan to kidnap me.

By then, I was curled up in the backseat, sobbing silently. Crispin was sending me somewhere and he hadn't even said goodbye. He'd lied to me... *again*. I sniffled and wiped my hand on my sleeve. Ben cast a glance back at me. He'd checked on me in the rear view mirror a couple times, but he hadn't said anything throughout the hour drive. He'd taken my phone and I didn't even know if I would have any clothes or the ability to take my exams.

"I am truly apologetic, Amina. However, I believe Barclay has your best interests at heart. Try not to kill Theo on the jet?"

"Screw you," I hissed.

"I'll talk to her," Theo said calmly. "I told him this would break her heart."

Ben's jaw tightened.

"Barclay's dealing with something much bigger than he realizes. He'll be lucky if he survives the summer. It's better that she knows the truth."

"Come on, Amina." Theo said, getting out of the car and opening the door, freeing me from the child locks. I didn't have the energy to run.

"What about my exams?" I whispered.

I didn't even know why I'd asked.

"I see Liberty has had an effect on you…" Ben grumbled. "Theodore will explain. Barclay has attended to your every need. I understand you're hurt but… you will be *safe*. I promise. It's my only chance of surviving Liberty."

"I don't want to spend the summer alone," I whispered.

Ben offered me a sympathetic look.

"Take her, Theo. The faster you get her out of here, the better."

Numb, I followed Theo onto the jet. I sat across from him and he immediately pulled a spliff from behind his ear. I hated him so much. Crispin's cousin looked too much like Crispin and now, I really hated Crispin.

"Want a puff?"

"I want the whole damn thing."

He handed it to me. "There."

I put it between my lips, but then I remembered the last time I'd smoked. Crispin had been there. I felt hurt. Angry. Betrayed.

"You kidnapped me," I snapped, taking the spliff out of my mouth.

"Yes. Sorry."

"Where are we going?"

"To your summer home. Crispin said he'd mentioned."

Now I was fuming. New Orleans. He was sending me to New Orleans alone with his stupid weed-addicted cousin.

"I hate him," I snapped. "I'm never going to forgive him for this. *Ever*."

"He still loves you, Amina," Theo said. "Trust me, Crispin still loves you."

"If he still loved me, he wouldn't have done this," I snapped.

And I meant every word of what I said. Theo sighed and puffed away. Enjoy your weed, Theo. The second we land this plane, I'm going to escape. I'm going to get back to Crispin Barclay and I'm going to kick my stupid boyfriend's ass.

THE END

Does she get her hands on Crispin again, or are they over for good?

Click here to order the next book:

Click here to order Book #5

About Jamila Jasper

The hotter and darker the romance, the better.

That's the Jamila Jasper promise.

If you enjoy sizzling multicultural romance stories that dare to *go there* you'll enjoy any Jamila Jasper title you pick up.

Open-minded readers who appreciate **shamelessly sexy romance novels** featuring black women of all shapes and sizes paired with smokin' hot white men are welcome.

Sign up for her e-mail list here to receive one of these FREE hot stories, exclusive offers and an update of Jamila's publication schedule:
bit.ly/jamilajasperromance

Get text message updates on new books:
https://slkt.io/gxzM

Extremely Important Links

ALL BOOKS BY JAMILA JASPER
https://linktr.ee/JamilaJasper
SIGN UP FOR EMAIL UPDATES
Bit.ly/jamilajasperromance
SOCIAL MEDIA LINKS
https://www.jamilajasperromance.com/
GET MERCH
https://www.redbubble.com/people/jamilajasper/shop
GET FREEBIE (VIA TEXT)
https://slkt.io/qMk8
READ SERIAL (NEW CHAPTERS WEEKLY)
www.patreon.com/jamilajasper

JAMILA JASPER

Diverse Romance For Black Women

More Jamila Jasper Romance

<u>Pick your poison...</u>

Delicious interracial romance novels for all tastes. Long novels, short stories, audiobooks and more.

Hit the link to experience my full catalog.

FULL CATALOG BY JAMILA JASPER:

https://linktr.ee/JamilaJasper

Patreon

13 SEASONS OF SERIAL CHAPTERS

NEW preview chapters published WEEKLY on my Patreon.

Read all 6 seasons of *Unfuckable* (Ben & Libby's story)…

Unfuckable

For a small monthly fee, you get exclusive access to over 375 chapters of my first completed bwwm dark and spicy serial romance, as well as the spin-off serial...

Despicable

The second serial, despicable has 300 chapters available for all Patreon subscribers to access instantly and... we officially have a **third completed spin-off bwwm romance series.**

And yes you get access to all of this at the $5/month tier with more benefits at more pricey tiers.

The third serial is about Clover + Thomas. Thomas has a shocking connection to a character in the second serial and Clover is an all-new African American female lead.

Powerless

This series has three *very long* "seasons" of chapters, the length of five full-length novels all-together.

You will probably have over three months of binge-reading before catching up to current content, making this one of the most 'bang for your buck' author Patreon subscriptions out there.

Don't take my word for it.

Check the post history:

www.patreon.com/jamilajasper

Patreon has more than the ongoing serial...

⚡ INSTANT ACCESS ⚡

- NEW merchandise tiers with **t-shirts, totes, mugs,** stickers and MORE!
- **FREE paperback** with all new tiers

- **FREE short story audiobooks** and audiobook samples when they're ready
- #FirstDraftLeaks of Prologues and first chapters **weeks** before I hit publish
- Behind the scenes notes
- Polls and story contribution
- Comments & LIVELY community discussion with likeminded interracial romance readers.

LEARN MORE ABOUT SUPPORTING A DIVERSE ROMANCE AUTHOR

www.patreon.com/jamilajasper

Thank You Kindly

Thank you to all my readers, new and old for your support with this new year.

I look forward to making 2023 an INCREDIBLE year for interracial romance novels. I want to thank you all for joining along on the journey.

www.patreon.com/jamilajasper

Thank you to my most supportive readers — my Patreon subscribers!:

Carla

Jonathan

Kelly

Jessica

Jasmine

DARSHELL

Dawn

Tiabuena3

Leigh

Yvonne

Ashlee

Crystal

Marshybabyyy

Shout

Quaniquequia

TK

Kayla

Shronda C.

Ma-Eyongerie

Kayla

Chantell

Kheiara

ophelia

Vickie

Cass

Kamil

Kaela

Love

Miryam

Charlene

Summer

Lola

Eryn

DD Davis

Symone

Deborah

Beatrice

Valescha

Khadija

makhalaab

Kaya

Glitter Garden

SavageSam

sybil arroyo

Ncsportsfan79

Jessica G.

Danielle

Yola

Joslin

Alexciz

Stacia

Ayanna

Asia

Hailey

Kaya

Nikki

Naomi O.

Jessica J

Chakiya

Noelle

kourtnee

Martha

Nikki Valentina

xjkpop

Valeria

BlkBae

SweetS

Msteeq

Rhonda

Darrah

Killa

Shavon

Misty

India

Kassandra

Imani

Nala

Chantell

Benvinda

Roger

Lexi B

Zapphire

Vbrooks

Tasha G

Kiera

Valencia

Stacy

YANITZA

Texansgurl76

Emma

Tinette

Jenny

Mariah

Nale

Tanisha

Trenita

Shelle

dulcemaria413

Shanice

Letarsha

Tania

Neeka

Julia

Linda

Lisa

Jiannie

Jillian

Tameka

Asia

Scarlette

Olwyn

R W

Fayefaefee

Brianna

Tiffany

Katie

Diamond

Kera

Tia

Love Reading

Dominique

Sheria

Jennifer

Georgette

Monique

Wendolyn

King Turtle22

Jessica

Nic M.

JustChill

DJC

Atira

TheeLastHokage

Yvonne

Chrissy

Janelle

Rian

LaRonda

LaRonda

Deanna

dlawson382

Jasmine

Haley

Belinda

Sercee

Yvonne

Jadelock

Farah

Tamiya

Quin

J.Payton

Geek Girl

Ashley

Rubi

Pilar

Sandra

Jurnee

Anni

Shannet

Joneesa

GlitzyHydra

Amanda

Barbara

Brianna

Jamica

Lyons

MARY ANN

Marketia

SarahD

LoverofHawaiiHearts

ceblue

Yolanda

MonaGirl Lewis

Dianna

Mary

amna

Nysha

fayola

Ty

Abria

Shyra

Andi-Mariee

Jamila

Naee's World

KEISHA

Jennett

Fredericka

Candece

Chante

Pholuv

Lydia A

Sabrina

JM

Jackie

Mo

Natrilly83

Ashaunte

Tolu

Margaret

Wendolyn

Lori

Dionne

ZLB

Kristina

Nicol

ELBERT

A. Harris

Jesi

Brenda

Desiree

Angela

Frances

LaShan

Only1ToniD

Debbie T.

Tiffanie

April L

shawnte

Kay

Lisema

Yvonne F

Natasha

Colleen

Julia

Amy

Jacklyn

Shyan R

Kiana B

Pearl

Javonda

Sheron

Maxine

Dash

Alicia

margaret

Love2Read

Juliette

Monica

Sandhya

MaryC

Trinity

Brittany

June

Ashleigh

Nene

Nene

Deborah

Nikki M

Dee

TyKira

Kimmey

Laytoya

Shel W

Arlene

Judith

Mary

Shanida

Rachel

Damzel

Ahnjala

Kenya

momo

BJ

Akeshia

Melissa

Tiffany

sherbear

Nini J

Curtresa

REGGIE A.

Ashley

Mia

Tink138110

Phia

Sharon

Charlotte

Assiatu C

Regina

Romanda

Catherine

Gaynor

BF

Perpetua

Tasha G

Henri Ann

sara

skkent

Rosalyn

Danielle

Deborah J

Kirsten

ANA

Taylor R.

Charlene

Louanna

Michelle

Tamika

Lauren

RoHyde

Natasha

Shekynah

Cassie

AnnaBooms

Keitheena

Nick R

Gennifer M

Rayna

Anton

Jaleda

Kimvodkna

JaTonn

Jazmine

Anoushka

Raynischa

Audrey

Valeria

Courtney

Donna

Patrisha

Jenetha

LaKisha J.

Ayana

Taylor

Christy

Monica

FreyaJo

GRACE

Kisha

Christine

Alexandra

Amber

Natasha

Stephanie

LaKisha

kristylove7

Cynthea

DENICE

Latoya

monifacd .

Doneishia

Mariah

Gerry

Yolanda T

Yolanda P

Susan D

Phyllis H

Alisa K

Daveena K

Desiree S

Kimberly B

Robin B

Gary S

Stephanie MG

Georgette A

Kathy

Marty

JanetDaniels

Megan

Shelle

Delores

Janet

Lydia

Phyllis

Freda

Charlott R

Join the Patreon Community.

Made in the USA
Columbia, SC
06 June 2024